AS OTHERS SEE US

As Others See Us

Alan Phillips

JANUS PUBLISHING COMPANY
London, England

First published in Great Britain 1994
by Janus Publishing Company
Duke House, 37 Duke Street
London W1M 5DF

Copyright © Alan Phillips 1994

British Library Cataloguing-in-Publication Data
A catalogue record for this book is available
from the British Library

ISBN 1 85756 100 7

Cover photos by Rob Stirling

Cover design by Optigraph

Printed and bound in England by
Antony Rowe Ltd, Chippenham, Wiltshire.

Chapter 1

'The trouble is I'm gay.' What the hell am I saying, he thought. 'The trouble is I'm gay,' and it wasn't even true, strictly speaking. He had never slept with another man or had sex in any other way with a man. At least, not since he was seventeen, and in the Fifties seventeen was very young. Mutual masturbation with a friend was not considered queer; gay was not used in that context in those days, it was just experimenting.

Here I am, he thought, standing in a pub that I have used regularly for the last few years, telling colleagues I am gay. I must be drunk. What did I expect them to do? Hug and kiss me or storm off out. Would I be able to face these people again? Would I ever want to? What do they care that I'm retiring. It's just another free drink to most of them.

Paul Green wondered how he would cope with retirement. He had volunteered for redundancy and at fifty-four had decided to draw his pension too. What else could he do – his confidence was shattered, and at his age, in an industry full of yuppies, nobody was going to look at him for future employment. The TV industry had been his life for the past thirty-two years and, although he felt himself lucky because he had always enjoyed his work, he had worked to live, not as some of his colleagues, lived to work. He had worked hard and often 'above and beyond the call of duty'; certainly he had made many sacrifices in the early stages of his career. And now it was over.

The television industry, like nearly all other businesses these days, was looking for ways to become more efficient and to streamline procedures. Savings needed to be made in all departments. This was the year that the applications to renew franchises had to be submitted. The winner would be the company with the highest bid who had also passed the quality threshold. To this end Paul's company had looked at its Sales and Marketing department to evaluate the benefits of merging that area with another company's Sales House. The benefits outweighed the continuing costs of an independent operation. That was when Paul decided to volunteer for redundancy.

The weekend was the Easter bank holiday and so, to begin with, the days seemed normal, but come Tuesday morning and Paul knew his retirement had started. He had always been a pragmatic person and, as he had been closely involved with the day-to-day running of the company, the merger had not been a surprise. In fact, it seemed inevitable.

Paul didn't feel a failure, as if he had been thrown on the scrap-heap. Although he had enjoyed work he was now looking forward to his leisure. He knew that young blood was required to carry through the reforms that were about to take place. The challenge of competitive media in the shape of satellite television, the impact on revenue that would be felt when Channel 4 took over selling their own airtime, and, of course, the dreaded Information Technology. He was going to relax and enjoy himself.

It didn't take long to realise that he had been missing so much. He was now able to listen to music, read books, go to the cinema, the theatre, to go shopping and to go for walks. All things that he enjoyed. Time was no longer a major factor in his life. After meeting deadlines on a daily basis, time was now irrelevant. The stress that had been building up over the last few years was gradually disappearing. Travel had always been Paul's favourite pastime and he was soon doing plenty of that. In the next eighteen months he was to visit Majorca, the Estoril coast of Portugal and the Canary Islands, with a few trips to the Midlands and the Cotswolds to see friends. The main event of the year was a tour around the Indian Ocean to the Seychelles and Mauritius. He booked with British Airways to stop on Mahé in the Seychelles for seven days, then on to Praslin for a few days before spending a week on La Digue, returning to Mahé for an overnight stay and the morning flight to Mauritius for two weeks. He didn't think when he set off in June that this would change his life again so soon.

The day looked as if it was going to be much the same as any other – the sun shone, and any cloud that may have been trying to block these beautiful clear skies was dispersed by a light breeze that came from the sea.

Paul awoke aware that this was his last day on Mahé and he must pack to go to Praslin. He had made up his mind to take only a sports bag with him while he was island-hopping, and to leave the rest of his luggage at the airport. He could collect that when he returned before flying to Mauritius. He showered and dressed and then went to breakfast. Breakfast was something he was going

7

to miss when he got home. Tropical fruit, croissants and pastries were a long way from the toast and coffee that he was used to. A taxi was due at nine-forty-five to take him to the airport. The fifteen-minute flight, in the sort of plane that some people would rather die than travel by, was an experience by itself – no more than a dozen seats. Paul didn't mind small aircraft and was looking forward to the trip.

He arrived at the airport, and, as is usual at airports, had to wait. Paul sat down and started to look for his book. He noticed a boy sitting on his own. He was about twenty-three to twenty-five years old, he had jet black hair and dark eyes. He was very handsome, the sort of Latin looks that Paul liked in a boy. Paul carried on looking for his book but wondering if the boy was going to Praslin, and trying to decide if he was English. Despite his looks, his way of dress for some reason looked English. He wondered if they would be staying at the same hotel. It was a possibility; there were not too many top-class hotels on Praslin. Paul was booked into La Reserve. An announcement was made telling passengers to board the plane. Paul found a single seat and fastened his seat-belt. The engines started and they were soon roaring down the runway for take-off. He had barely a chance to look down at the islands below, some of which were nature reserves, before they were landing. They jumped from the plane and waited for the luggage to be unloaded. When it arrived they were escorted to taxis for the journey to the hotels. The boy shared a cab with Paul.

'Hello,' said Paul, 'are you staying at La Reserve?'

'No, I'm staying at the Meridian. It's just near La Reserve, which is why I'm sharing a cab with you, I suppose. I hope you don't mind,' he said.

8

'Of course not. It's nice to have some company, even if it is only for a short while.'

'Are you on your own?' asked the boy. 'I know what that can be like. I've travelled on my own quite a lot. People always think something's wrong with you.'

'Yes, that's true. Yes, I am on my own. I thought I would try to see as many of the islands as possible while I'm here,' said Paul.

They made small talk for the rest of the journey, but Paul was too fascinated by the boy to remember a word that was said. The drive took about forty minutes across the centre of the island, passing the Valley of Mai, the home of the black parrot and the coco de mer. They turned the next corner and the boy said, 'We're nearly at my hotel, perhaps we might bump into each other again.' The taxi stopped and he got out. With a wave and a smile he was gone.

Paul sat back thinking, was this the companion that he had always looked for on his travels? He would see.

The taxi turned into the grounds of La Reserve and continued to drive for a quarter of a mile before pulling up at the reception area. The first impression was wonderful. The buildings were all a chalet style with thatched roofs and looked very large. Paul checked in and was shown across the gardens and along by the beach to his chalet. This was to be his home for the next four days. This had to be paradise. The view of the mountains behind him was stunning. The trees, all sorts of trees, rolled down the mountainside to the water's edge. No promenade here. Along the beach palm trees threw a soft shadow over the white sands, coconuts hanging precariously from the tops of the trees. Paul had seen a notice hammered into the ground saying BEWARE OF FALLING COCONUTS; he had thought it was a joke. He

9

changed his mind when a thud behind him made him turn to see a dent in the sand that looked like a bomb crater, made by just such a falling coconut.

His chalet was very large. In the main room was a double bed shrouded with a mosquito net, a bedside table with a lamp and a telephone on it. Across the room was a writing desk, two armchairs and a wardrobe with plenty of space for his clothes. The wall was decorated with one picture, a print of Van Gogh's *Sunflowers*. The second room had been divided into two, part was the bathroom with all of the usual facilities, and a kitchen, for want of a better word. In the kitchen was a fridge, a mini-bar and equipment to make tea or coffee plus the necessary crockery. The patio had chairs, sun loungers with mattresses, and a table. There was no ceiling. The thatched roof was like an umbrella covering the entire building. It was all very different from hotels in Europe, but wonderful nevertheless. The wooden shutters on the windows gave the place a French Colonial feel. Paul started to unpack, thinking about the boy . . .

Paul had been looking for a companion all his life. He did not feel lonely, but sometimes very alone. He knew he was missing out on a lot. Experiences had to be shared. It was no fun going to the theatre if you couldn't argue a point or rave about the show that you had just seen. It was the same on holiday: to explore the town or to find a restaurant where the locals eat and try the national food was not a lot of fun on your own. Sharing brought things to life.

Paul was naturally very shy and this didn't help in trying to form relationships. As a kid he had always felt mixed up. He didn't understand his feelings. He had always had many girlfriends when he was at school, he knew about the birds and the bees but he did not have any feelings for girls. He did, however, have feelings for boys. He liked them. He wanted to be with them; have secrets with them; have fun with them. He knew though, even at that age, it was not what other boys wanted. He didn't understand.

Paul left school at sixteen. It had been a nightmare. Everybody was older than him and certainly seemed more worldly. He was shy and embarrassed with them, having nothing in common with them, even the boys nearest his own age. He found them coarse and vulgar. It wasn't that he was a prude, he just found it all so unnecessary.

Steve was a boy Paul knew from the youth club. Steve was older than Paul and Paul had not been friendly with him any more than he had with anybody else. It was a surprise therefore when one day Steve knocked at Paul's door. Steve said he had seen Paul at the club and had found out where he lived. Paul invited him in and introduced Steve to his parents. They went to Paul's room and played records and talked. Steve had already left school and was working in the West End. Paul had been to London, but not very often, and so when Steve suggested that they go into town one evening Paul immediately agreed. It soon became a regular thing. Steve and Paul would catch the train to Waterloo, walk across the bridge to the Embankment and then they would walk to Soho and spend time in the coffee bars which were opening up everywhere in those days. Sometimes when they both had enough money they would go to a show, usually a musical, but sometimes a play. Occasionally they would go to the local dance hall. Paul enjoyed this as it gave him an easy way to meet other people. Girls. Mostly though, they would wonder around town. One night they went back to Paul's home earlier than usual. Neither

11

of them had any money and it was getting boring just walking about. Paul's parents were out and so Paul went to make some supper. When Paul returned to the lounge Steve had started to undress. He had already taken off his shirt and trousers. Paul was sixteen – he didn't know about homosexuality, he didn't even know the word. But of course, like all boys he had learnt to masturbate and he had experienced an orgasm. Steve was now naked. He pulled Paul towards him and unzipped his trousers. It was not long before both boys were playing with each other. To Paul it was just a bit of fun, doing what he had done loads of times by himself, with somebody else. He wanted to talk about it afterwards.

These meetings became a regular event and the sexual activity became more daring. 'You suck my dick and I'll suck yours.' Paul realised that what he thought of as harmless fun Steve was taking more seriously. Steve tried to encourage Paul to experiment, but Paul wasn't interested and said no. Gradually Steve stopped coming round.

Years later Paul realised that this was his first homosexual experience, although he certainly did not know that at the time.

The three years that Paul spent in the RAF had made little change in him. At twenty-two he was still immature and very naive. It was now in the sixties. Not the time to be innocent. This meant for Paul that he had to bluff his way through life. He had reached the age where it was expected that he would have had experience. He hadn't. It was too late now to ask questions. To avoid getting into a situation he couldn't control, Paul became very distant. It seemed to be the answer. Don't get too familiar, keep your distance with everybody and you won't make a fool of yourself. It worked. He put all of his energy into his job. If he was asked to socialise in the evening, he made an excuse not to go. However, as he became more established within the firm he did on occasions join in the celebrations. It was soon accepted that Paul was always good for a round at a leaving party or birthday, but he would always leave early and never get too involved. Paul was well aware that the other men in the office talked about him and wondered why he didn't have a girlfriend. He tried to be friendly with them, but he knew that he wanted something different. He had to be careful and play by the rules. Not to be too friendly, this was considered non-macho. Real men didn't behave like that. They talked about football and women and effed and blinded all the time. He kept his distance. He had long ago realised that the only women that he could relax with were married women. He did not have to prove anything to them, let their husbands do that. Paul was also beginning to face the fact, in looking at men, that he was having fantasies about them becoming his mythical friend. Sex didn't come into his fantasies. He knew that his sex life was a mess. He would visit public lavatories where queers gathered to masturbate and pick up men. Sometimes if he had more to drink than he intended, and so was not in control, he would stretch these visits to longer than was necessary. While watching the other men he would be doing the same thing to himself. He felt dirty and hated himself. He hated what he was doing but he knew that he could never be an active homosexual. It was wrong, it was against the way he had been brought up, and at the time it was against the law. He knew it would be unfair to get married, although he was certain that a number of marriages did exist when one partner was gay. Paul continued to lead his celibate and independent life.

13

He became more successful at work and enjoyed what he was doing. He portrayed the bachelor image without appearing to be gay. Not uncommon, of course, look at the adverts in the papers. 'Gay, straight-acting/looking seeks similar.' It would be so easy if that was what he wanted.

Paul had always tried to keep his work and home life separate. At work, if he went for a drink he was still the boss. At home he tried to be one of the boys. Still playing by the rules. Usually things were fine, everyone knew that he lived on his own and accepted his life for what it was. Paul liked to go for a drink at the local pub and knew a lot of people to talk to there. He nearly got himself into a hole once when a guy he knew tried to talk him into a cruise as a holiday. 'I'm sure you would like it, and we could go together.' He was divorced and looking for a partner to help him chase women for two weeks. Paul managed to convince him that he didn't like boats and he would probably be sick all the time.

Paul had been going on holiday on his own since a disastrous two weeks he had spent at a holiday camp when he was seventeen. That year he was part of a group who regularly went dancing together, but who were not necessarily couples. Paul agreed to go away with Ken, also part of the group. Ken was a lot older than Paul and interested in only one thing: getting into bed with as many different girls as he could. Paul was incapable of joining Ken on these conquests and consequently spent most of the time by himself. From then on he decided that he would be more selective with whom he went on holiday.

It was when he was on holiday that Paul became aware of his need for friendship. He would watch people at the airport to see if any were travelling alone and if so try to

14

find out if they were on his flight. Even if they were, they usually had someone to meet them at the destination. Not many people actually travelled by themselves. He certainly had never found one. He had dinner alone, sat around the pool alone, had a drink at the bar alone. People went on holiday in couples and wanted it to stay that way. Paul had noticed that if a couple did speak to anyone it was always another couple, to keep the balance. If a foursome had gone away together they generally had enough troubles of their own without being bothered by a weirdo who travelled solo. 'What is the matter with him anyway, nobody travels alone. If we start to talk to him we'll have him hanging around all the time. We'll never get rid of him.' The problems of the single traveller.

Paul would sometimes feel very sorry for himself, knowing that there wouldn't be any love in his life. What he would like was a platonic relationship, but he doubted that that was possible with a man. He began to wonder if one-night stands were not the answer to his sex life but he knew that they were not. He had to be sincere. He had not been the sort of person to say 'it's only a bit of fun,' at least, not for the last thirty-seven years since he had been friends with Steve.

Now he was unpacking in the Seychelles, thinking, as he had done in his twenties, about a boy who was half his age.

Paul, who had already dressed for the evening, decided to wander through the gardens before he made his way to the bar for a pre-dinner drink. As always at this time of night it was black. The sun set at six o'clock and it was dark; no evening. The paths were well lit and so it was still possible to see how the gardens were laid out and to appreciate how magnificent they must look in the daylight. He finally arrived at the bar and ordered a margarita, a drink that he had discovered on Mahé: tequila, cointreau, lemon juice and ice with a rim of salt around a well chilled glass. The bar was not yet full; a couple sitting on the veranda with a drink which had more fruit and umbrellas in the glass than alcohol. They looked happy – it was something they would never do at home, order a drink like that.

Paul sipped his margarita and wallowed in the peacefulness that surrounded him. Even a balmy summer's evening in England was not the same. Here you could totally relax; perhaps because the distant sounds of aircraft and other traffic would not disturb the tranquillity of the islands.

A few more guests arrived at the bar for the first drink of the evening, mainly Italians. That shattered the peace. Paul had noticed on Mahé that Italian tourists were plentiful, and they always seemed to talk at once. Three English couples and some French people joined them. The restaurant was next to the bar, but on this evening they were eating on the jetty, which ran from the dining room out to sea. It was to be a Gala Dinner. A six-course Creole speciality: soup to start, followed by a fish dish which was very spicy. The meat was also cooked with a number of herbs and spices. It seemed to have been cooked in an oven very slowly and tasted delicious. After all that spice a sorbet was served to clear the palate, and was most welcome. A dessert with cheese and biscuits came next and coffee and petits fours to round it all off. A gala meal indeed.

After he had finished his meal Paul went for a nightcap. It was to be a big night as the local band were playing for the guests' entertainment and for the hotel staff, judging by the number of them in or around the bar. Unfortunately they were trying to be too western, playing poor imitations of American hits instead of what they knew best. Paul thought most of the guests would rather have had local music played to which they could dance. He went to bed.

The next morning after breakfast Paul went to reception to ask about any walks he might be able to take.

'Good morning. Can you tell me if I can walk to the hotel Meridian from here?' asked Paul.

'Yes, it is not a problem, but if you want you can get a taxi from here. If you prefer to walk, go to the main entrance and turn left, keep walking straight ahead until you pass the Medical Centre. It is then on your right; it is not far.'

He thanked the receptionist and set off to the hotel where he knew that the boy was staying. Paul had made up his mind to go into the hotel on the pretext of looking around with the view of staying there another time – hoping that he might see him. As Paul turned into the grounds he saw a familiar figure walking towards him.

'Hello, remember me? I shared a taxi with you yesterday from the airport.'

'Yes, of course I do. It's nice to see you again,' said Paul.

'My name is Richard Carter.' He held out his hand in the traditional greeting.

'How do you do. My name is Paul Green. Have you settled in at the Meridian?'

'Yes, it's fine. What about you, you're staying at La Reserve aren't you? What's that like?'

'Fine. In fact, superb,' said Paul. 'Where were you off to when we met? I don't want to hold you up.'

'Not at all, I was only going to the village to buy some

17

tee-shirts, they're very cheap and don't take up much room when you pack to go home,' said Richard. 'Why don't you come along with me, it's not far and perhaps you would allow me to buy you a drink at the beach?'

'That sounds like the best offer I'm ever going to get today,' smiled Paul. 'I'd be delighted to join you.'

'You're quite sure? You were going to the hotel when I saw you.'

'I can look round the hotel any time, I'd much rather come with you.' They strolled off towards the village, avoiding the potholes and bikes.

'You seem to know your way around. Have you been here before?' asked Paul.

'Yes, this is my secret hideaway. I first came here five years ago when I was twenty. I was spellbound. It was so different to anything I had even seen in my squalid life in London,' said Richard.

'Squalid,' said Paul. 'How is life squalid?'

'I'm only joking. Don't take everything I say too seriously. I suppose what I really mean is the routine of it all. Travelling to work on the tube every day, doing the same thing all the time. You know what us youngsters are like, get bored with anything after a few days.' He laughed.

'I expect the locals here think this is boring and would love to go England and see London. We all take our lives for granted and it's not until we stand back and look at things dispassionately that we realise that we're not too badly off. What do you do in the evening, for example? The sun sets at six and it's pitch dark: no cinemas, no theatres, even the bars seem to close. At least they did on Mahé,' said Paul.

'Of course you are right, but it's nice to have a moan

now and again,' grinned Richard. 'Perhaps I need someone like you to keep me on the straight and narrow.'

'I'm sure you're perfectly capable of looking after yourself. What do you do for a living?' said Paul.

'I work at a photographer's in Bond Street. In fact, I part-own it. Chris, a friend I was at university with, and I decided to set up a business together. I often feel a bit of a fraud, I run the day-to-day things, but Chris has the talent. We're doing quite well,' said Richard.

'What sort of pictures does he take?' asked Paul. 'What is your client base?'

'Mainly actors and models. They're always needing updates for their portfolios. You know what it's like – the face and fashion changes and so the model or actor needs new pictures.'

'Interesting. It must be fairly profitable if you can come here every year.'

'Ah,' said Richard. 'I didn't say that I came here every year, only that my first visit was about five years ago.'

'I'm sorry,' said Paul, blushing a little. 'Is that the beach where you are going to buy me a drink? Only now I think this one is on me. I have enjoyed your company, Richard, you are a very pleasant young man, not like some I have known.' Careful, thought Paul, don't want to scare him away.

'That's very noble of you, Paul. I never refuse a drink from anyone,' he was grinning. 'The feeling is mutual, I have enjoyed your company too. I would like to think we could see more of each other over the next few days. How long are you here for?'

'I'm here until the end of the week, then I'm going to La Digue for a week before going back to Mahé and then on to Mauritius for two weeks.'

Richard was killing himself with laughter.

'You think I'm rich, and you've just told me an itinerary that I would kill for.'

'Yes, I suppose it does sound a bit grand. I have only myself to please, so why not.'

'Why not indeed?' said Richard wistfully.

Paul ordered a couple of beers.

'Well, you know all about me, now about you. What do you do for a living?' said Richard.

Paul got the distinct feeling that Richard didn't want to say too much about himself. It was as though he wanted to change the subject.

'As a matter of fact, I'm retired. An early retirement I hasten to add, although I don't think I need to, or at least I hope I don't,' smiled Paul.

'It would never have crossed my mind that you were of retiring age,' grinned Richard. 'What made you take such a big step?'

'Lots of things were changing at work and so I volunteered for redundancy when I had the opportunity and decided to take my pension too. I'm not married, my parents are dead, I don't have any brothers or sisters, so I don't have any family responsibilities. I can do what I like. I felt that to retire from normal work at my age was a good time for me to do what I wanted to do and to see the things that I wanted. I like travelling and I like theatres and cinema, I have found plenty to fill my time. Why not enjoy life while you are still young enough to do so? Providing that you have enough money, of course,' said Paul.

'It sounds pretty lonely to me,' said Richard.

Strange how he should pick up on that.

'Sometimes I am alone a lot, but not really lonely,' said Paul.

'Where do you live – in London?' asked Richard.

'Yes, in Hounslow, West London. What about you, where do you live?'

'I've got a flat in Chelsea, just off the King's Road. I was born in Sussex, a village called Frogham, which nobody's ever heard of.'

Again changing the subject, Richard asked, 'Have you ever been married?'

'No.' There was a long pause in the conversation as though Richard expected more of an answer. 'What about you? Have you got a girlfriend or a wife that you've run away from for two weeks?' said Paul.

'No wife,' smiled Richard. 'I did have a girlfriend, Sarah. We were together for two years, but we split up some time ago.'

'Why, after so long?'

'I think we were too young, I'm only twenty-five now. We were working together at the studio and I think it became a bit overpowering. We both needed some space. We're still friends.' Richard turned to Paul and said, 'Now I am the same as you. Living on my own. It appears from a survey that I was reading before I came away that it's becoming more and more common for people to live as single units. Being independent is in fashion at the moment.'

'Living by ourselves, no family. Is it independence or is it selfishness, I wonder?' said Paul.

'You could be right.'

'You were saying about Chris and the business when fashion changes. I remember a photograph my mother had taken of me as a child. It still sends shivers down my back now. I was about four or five, standing on a chair dressed in a sailor's suit with long blond ringlets, can you imagine? I used to plead with my mother to get rid of it, but she wouldn't. The best I managed was for the picture to go to my parents' bedroom.'

Richard was laughing. 'I can just see you camping it up on a chair in a sailor's suit. Hello, sailor.' Paul grimaced.

'I'm sorry, I shouldn't have said that – I don't know you that well.'

'Don't worry. It's the first time in years that I've been embarrassed by that picture,' said Paul.

'Do you miss your colleagues from the office?' said Richard.

'Not really. They weren't friends, only workmates. We didn't have a lot in common. I don't know if I mentioned it but I worked in the TV industry and that can be pretty fast moving. I've been out of it for over a year. I doubt if I would have even work in common with them now, but I still see a few people for a drink,' said Paul. 'When you asked me if I was married just now, I had the feeling that you were waiting for more of an answer.'

'Was it so obvious?' said Richard blushing. 'It is that the one-word answer does beg another one-word question. Why? I'm sorry, I don't mean to pry, you don't have to tell me anything. It's that I feel comfortable talking to you and it seemed a natural thing to ask. You look so married. I can picture you with a wife and two point five children. When you said you weren't married I thought you might have been a widower, even divorce wasn't the first thing to cross my mind.'

Paul while listening to Richard had been wondering what to say.

'I'm not gay, or at least I don't think I am.'

'Phew, that's a relief,' grinned Richard. 'I wouldn't have known which way to turn if you were.'

'Cute,' said Paul feeling more relaxed with Richard than he had with anybody in years.

22

'It's funny,' said Richard, 'at home all of my friends and most of the people I come into contact with at the studio are all aged between twenty-two and thirty-five, I'm afraid that I tend to think of anyone who's over forty as dull and boring and not in touch with what is going on today. I don't feel that way with you. I feel we're both on the same level and not as though I'm having a drink with my father.'

'That's because I have never had the responsibilities of a married man. I'm still a kid at heart. I feel like a man of twenty-five, and if you say I'm twenty-five you can have me, I'll give you a smacking.' They both laughed and finished their drinks.

'Hadn't we better start back,' said Paul.

Chapter 2

Richard had spent a lot of time with Paul over the last three days. He was wondering if it was a good thing. They had been on a trip to one of the outer islands for the day. They had had fun. It was all so innocent. They had been swimming and played about on the beach, sunbathed and went swimming again. They had taken some food and managed to find a shop where they could buy a few beers. Paul asked Richard to rub some sun cream on his back; it was strange. As soon as Richard touched him he felt Paul stiffen almost as if he felt it was sexy. He had caught Paul watching him when he thought he could not be seen, and he felt his eyes on him when he was changing to go swimming. Richard knew he possessed good looks and a good body, he also knew that he drove gays mad when he was showing off on the beach. He was sure that Paul fancied him, but he was equally sure that Paul was straight. This was something different; Paul wanted company – he was lonely, despite what he had told Richard. Paul needed a person to talk to and for someone to talk to him, no commitments, no strings on either side. They had talked a lot and Richard thought he knew Paul pretty well. He liked him and he felt comfortable with him, more than could be said of his usual companions. Paul was the sort of person that let life pass them by for some reason. They devote so much time to work or other interests that before they realise it they are forty-five with a very empty life. Now Paul had retired he found that he needed social skills that he had not needed for the last twenty years. He had to make small talk with people, he had to communicate with people and he found it difficult. Perhaps that was why he got on with Richard, because he was so much younger. Paul would therefore think that Richard was about as experienced as he was himself about life. How wrong he was, thought Richard. People like Paul were popular with the crowd that they did mix with, because they were usually macho in a non-aggressive way and nobody felt pressurised socially by them.

Richard kept thinking about how this was going to end. Once the holiday was over, then what? Paul was certainly going to want a phone number or an address that could be used to contact him. As they both lived in London he was bound to suggest they meet. Richard's acquaintances would hardly appeal to Paul. It was going to be a problem. He would worry about it when they got back from La Digue.

He had to get ready, he was having dinner tonight with Paul at a restaurant at South Point, a good Creole restaurant on the far side of the island. Paul had arranged for a taxi to pick him up at six-thirty then to go to La Reserve to pick up Paul.

Richard finished dressing and was still thinking about what he should do about his friendship with Paul. It occurred to him for the first time that he did look on this episode as a friendship; unusual for him. He would get Paul to say how he felt things should continue once back in London. Maybe Paul had no intention of staying in contact with him. Paul could be as worried about being seen at home with a twenty-five year old as Richard was about Paul meeting any of his friends. It will all end at the airport when we go home, thought Richard.

The taxi arrived on time. Richard told the driver to pick up Paul at La Reserve. Paul was waiting as usual like an eager schoolboy. It was this sort of thing that puzzled Richard.

'Hi, did you manage to get your letter written?' asked Paul.

'Yes, it was only a line to Chris to say when I would be available for work.'

'When you are available for work? That's a funny way of saying that your holiday is over,' said Paul.

Richard looked quickly at Paul to see if he could read his face, to know what he meant by saying that. 'I suppose it did sound a bit melodramatic but I'm taking a couple of extra days when I get home. I always find it difficult to go straight from a holiday to a normal working routine,' said Richard.

The taxi pulled up at the restaurant. Paul paid the driver and they went in. Like all restaurants in the Seychelles, the aroma of newly picked flowers was in the air. The tables were covered with petals, a centrepiece made up of local flora sat in the middle of each table. Most of the tables were taken but Paul and Richard still managed to be shown to a table with a splendid view of the village below and the sea. At this time of night the village was lit up and the church and the community centre stood out from the houses as the focal points of the village. The sea was only a dark rumbling noise in the background. Occasionally a white line of surf could be seen breaking over the rocks at the edge of the lagoon.

They ordered their meal and a bottle of wine – not a usual practice as wine was so expensive on any island in the Seychelles. As they were eating Richard said, 'What are we going to do when this holiday is over, Paul?'

'What do you mean? Do about what?'

'About us,' said Richard.

Paul laughed. 'You sound like something out of *Brief Encounter*, a film of the Forties with Trevor Howard. I don't suppose that you remember it.'

'Of course I've heard of it,' said Richard laughing too. 'You know what I mean, we've seen a lot of each other here and when we get back to London it's back to the real world.' Richard was looking quite uncomfortable, thought Paul. 'We lead different lives, I just thought . . . Oh, I don't know what I thought,' said Richard.

'Richard, I am not going to embarrass you in front of your friends. I admit I've had a wonderful holiday and a lot of that has been to do with you, and I'd certainly like to see you again when we get home. I'm sure it's not beyond us to make some arrangements to see each other. What do you think?'

'The truth.'

'I thought we'd always been truthful.'

'I hope we can go on being friends as we are now, come what may. But I'm not sure that it's possible,' said Richard.

'Why, because I'm old enough to be your father, or is it because you think I'm gay and only want to get into your bed?'

Richard laughed. 'You don't know how funny that is. No, I don't think you're gay, and I've had more experience of the ways of the world than you. I know what I'm talking about. It's not because you're fifty-five either. As you said once, you feel like a twenty-five year old, remem-

27

ber. I believe that when we get home we'll both fall into our separate routines, and, like all holidays, this will just be a memory. A very pleasant memory, but that's all,' said Richard.

'I often come up to town, I could easily come to your studio.'

'No!' cried Richard.

'What's the matter? OK, if not at the office, at your flat, now that you're not with Sarah,' said Paul.

'Let's change the subject, we're sure to think of something. We've got four more days on La Digue yet.'

They finished the meal in relative silence. Paul did not understand what was going on, but it was obvious that Richard didn't want him to be part of his life in London.

They said goodnight from the taxi, and agreed to meet at the harbour in the morning for the journey to La Digue.

Paul slept badly that night. He kept thinking of Richard's reaction to his suggestion that they meet in London. There was something wrong and he could not quite put his finger on it. Paul liked Richard; he got on well with him. He knew that the difference between their ages was a little odd, but so what? He had never enjoyed a holiday so much. He had never had a friend to whom he felt so close. Paul wanted to tell Richard more about himself, how he felt, and how he would like them to continue to be friends. He knew it was too early to say anything – it would only lead to more misunderstandings. Richard was between girlfriends at the moment and Paul was sure that with Richard's looks and charm it would not be long before he found another one. Deep down Paul thought that Richard did think that he was trying to get into his trousers. He knew Richard must have seen him looking at him when he was on the beach. He had to have noticed the times that Paul had touched him. Paul had put his arm around Richard's shoulder and had grabbed his arm. He didn't mean anything by it. It just increased his feel-good factor. Perhaps Richard thought he would be an embarrassment. After all, Richard had a good job in a business that was made up of trendy people who were full of self-confidence and assertiveness, not exactly how Paul would describe himself. He hoped that the next week on La Digue would go well. He would be on his guard not to be too pushy about meeting in London. Maybe he could get Richard to come to his place for the weekend now and again. That way they would be away from Richard's friends and so avoid any problems.

He finally fell asleep and had an erotic dream about Richard.

The next morning Paul set off for the harbour. He had got a ticket and, as far as he knew, the boats left every hour on the hour. People were beginning to arrive already, although it was only nine-forty. Not Richard. Those that had arrived were from the hotels. None of the locals who used the ferry daily ever arrived until just as the boat was about to leave. La Digue was a small island and supplies had to be ferried in regularly. It was also an island where other islanders went when they got time off. The fishing was good and so was the diving. So it was not a surprise to see a cook from La Reserve waiting at the harbour. The guide books said that the transport was primitive. Bicycle, ox-cart for the tourists, or walking. The ox-cart took guests to the hotels and day-trippers round the island.

'Looking for company? I'm free for a couple of hours.' Richard said sheepishly, 'I'm sorry for last night. I was being a prat, I don't know why.'

29

'Forget it,' said Paul, unable to mask his pleasure now that Richard had arrived.

'I'll try to make it up to you while we're here,' said Richard. 'The boat has just moored, so let's go if we want to get a seat. I understand that these boats get fairly full with the natives, who all turn up at the last minute.'

'Yes, that's what I've heard.'

Although the trip was only about an hour, if the sea was rough that could seem a lifetime. They had been going about fifteen minutes when the wind got stronger and with it the swell came up. Paul had not been on a boat since he was a kid and that had been rough too. He had said he would never go on a boat again.

Paul looked at Richard; he didn't look too bad but he seemed to be hoping that this would not last long. They smiled at each other and survived. They came into La Digue harbour without any problems, which was a relief. Paul thought they might have had trouble as it was still very choppy. They climbed off the boat and instantly felt better. Richard looked around and pointed to a girl who was dressed in some sort of uniform. 'She must be our guide. Let's go and introduce ourselves,' he said. They walked over to the girl. 'I'm Richard Carter and this is Paul Green. We're staying at the Island Lodge Hotel. Are you with West Island Tours?'

'Yes, I am your representative, my name is Marna.' She held out her hand in greeting. Richard and Paul shook hands with her and said how pleased they were to meet her.

Marna motioned to a boy who was standing nearby to take the bags. 'If you would like to follow me I will take you to the hotel; we are going in the ox-cart. It's not very far.'

Paul and Richard climbed on to the cart. The boy who

had taken their bags was also the driver. He perched on a bar which crossed the harness of the cart and with a flick of his whip they were off. The cart trundled down the road finding every pothole it could. This is the last time I do this, thought Paul. Not only is it uncomfortable, it stinks to high heaven.

They were welcomed at the hotel, as usual in those parts, with a non-alcoholic cocktail. They registered and were shown to chalets which were next to one another. By now both Paul and Richard had a good tan and so didn't have to be careful in the sun. They stripped off and went to explore before it got dark. They walked along the beach. The first building that they came to was the restaurant; next to that was a swimming pool, very large, very blue, and looking very inviting. At the far end of the pool was a snack bar and a shop selling postcards, books and all the usual things sold in hotel shops. What they both wanted was a drink. The bar was beside the pool, two sides faced out to the terrace and the other two faced in towards the pool. Paul and Richard dived in and swam across to the bar. It was wonderful. They ordered a couple of beers from the barman, who was called Sotto. They asked him if there were many guests staying at the hotel at the moment. He said not too many but that they did get a lot of day-trippers who had lunch there and drinks. Sotto asked how long they were staying and then asked Richard if Paul was his father. Paul laughed, but Richard was quite annoyed. Paul explained that they were friends who had met on Praslin and decided to spend time together on La Digue.

'That is good,' said the barman. 'It would be a pity if two nice Englishman were to be on the island on their own.'

Richard calmed down as he realised that the barman

31

had made an innocent remark. He was just a kid, why would he try to imply any innuendo. Richard reacts in a very strange way sometimes, thought Paul – all over nothing. They finished their drinks and continued to explore the grounds. Apart from the snack bar at the back of the pool there wasn't much more to see. A room upstairs that had some big, comfortable-looking armchairs, a television set and a pool table. Next to the pool was the diving centre which was run by David. They would get to know a lot about David during their stay at Island Lodge.

They strolled back to the chalets and downed another couple of beers. It was now dark; nothing to do except drink. After dinner they stayed in the bar until about eleven o'clock. They went to bed agreeing that tomorrow they would try to walk round the island. It was possible, they had been told.

Paul slept better that night; he felt that his friendship with Richard had returned to the way it was before any talk of meeting in London had taken place, a conversation which had created a tense atmosphere.

The next morning Paul and Richard, dressed in shorts, tee-shirts and trainers, set off to walk round the island. They had got a map from Marna and had decided to walk back to the harbour and in effect walk clockwise. They had soon passed through the village and were on their own. The scenery was, as usual, breathtaking. After they had been walking for about an hour they came across a beach that Marna had marked on the map as being a good beach for swimming and for diving. It was getting very hot and they both felt like a beer and a swim. They stopped. The sea looked so inviting that Paul said he was going swimming. He stripped off and went down the beach to paddle. He could see something in the water, but it was too far for him to make out what it was. He called to Richard.

'What do you make of that?' he asked, pointing out to sea.

'I think it's probably a diver. I think that looks like a snorkel sticking out of the water,' said Richard.

'The first person we've seen in over an hour and they're still miles away. I'm going for a swim. Nothing too energetic, I'm too old,' said Paul.

'Nonsense, you've got the body of someone ten years younger than you,' said Richard.

'Yes, that still makes it twenty years older than yours, so don't try any races. I can't take it,' said Paul.

'OK, dad. I won't show you up.'

Paul swam off along the coast. Richard dived in and followed him. He soon caught up with him and they began playing about, a lot of pushing and pulling under the water, a lot of body contact. Is it deliberate or am I being paranoid, thought Richard.

They came from the sea and dried off in the sun. It soon got too hot to lie in the open so they moved back under the trees. While they were relaxing with a not-so-cold beer Richard saw the diver walking from the sea.

'Look, here comes our mystery object from the sea, he must have had enough.' They watched him as he walked up the beach. Paul realised that although they could see him, he could not see them under the trees. He stopped and shrugged his air tanks off and unzipped his wet suit. He peeled off the suit and was completely naked. Richard was watching Paul. He could not take his eyes from the diver. Paul felt Richard looking at him.

'It's not the sort of thing that you see every day in London, is it,' he laughed.

'It's all right, Paul. I don't mind. I can imagine what

it's like when you've been on your own for as long as you have. If you ever want to talk, you can, you know. You might find me a very understanding listener.'

'No, I'm fine,' said Paul. 'I must be turning into a dirty old man.' They sat in silence for a while. Then Richard said, 'Come on, let's carry on with our trek. We can't stay here all day.'

They both got up and, making sure that they had picked up any rubbish, set off again to walk round the island.

Later that day when they had returned to the hotel Paul was alone in his chalet. What a fool I am, he thought. How could I have been so stupid as to leer over that boy like that? I thought I had got over that sort of thing. Visiting public loos to watch other men playing with themselves. Damn. Richard is such a nice guy, intelligent, well-mannered and good fun to be with. I was beginning to think that I might have found someone that I could have as a friend, no strings, even back in London. If I carry on like that I'll blow it because he will think I'm a fairy. Well, what's done is done.

Paul went to bed.

The next couple of days Paul and Richard were hardly ever apart, except when they went to bed. The incident on the beach with the diver was not mentioned and it appeared to have made no difference to Richard's attitude towards Paul. They went to the harbour and hired a boat to go sailing. It was the perfect place to sail in a lazy non-competitive way. The boatman was only about Richard's age and they got on well. They stopped at a small village and had lunch. Paul asked the boatman to join them. He was very flattered to be asked and readily accepted. His name was Harry and he told Paul and Richard that he had lived on the islands all of his life but that one day he wanted to go to Europe. They chatted over lunch and then set sail for a beach that Harry said was the best on the island. They arrived, and what Harry had said was true. Miles of white sand, the sea breaking gently onto the beach, the trees and shrubs spread along the coast. Harry anchored the boat and they all went swimming. Harry was an excellent swimmer and diver. He would dive down to the ocean bed and come back with some shells and rocks that neither Richard nor Paul had seen the like of before. When they moved off Paul went to Richard and put his arm round his shoulder.

He said, 'Richard, this has been a perfect day. I would never have done this if I hadn't met you. You'll never know how grateful I am to you. Even if we don't see each other again I want you to know that I will never forget you, as you've given me so much pleasure.' Paul stood up.

'Well, that was quite a speech. I'm sure we'll be able to come to some understanding so that we can see each other again. We still have a couple of days here yet, so let's enjoy them. I don't want to think about London and the work I have to go back to,' said Richard.

They spent the rest of the trip sunbathing.

The last day had arrived, or at least the last full day. They were leaving the island the next day to fly from Praslin to Mahé. Paul awoke early. The sun was already feeling hot. He dressed and went to call for Richard to go to breakfast. He went to his chalet and knocked at the door.

'Is that you, Paul? Come in. The door's open; I won't be long.' Paul went inside. Richard was still in the shower. Paul sat down on the bed.

'How did you sleep, Paul? OK?'

35

'Yes,' said Paul. 'Better than the other night.'

'What happened the other night?' asked Richard.

'I felt such a fool for the way I behaved over the diver. I couldn't sleep for wondering what you must have thought of me.'

'I told you, don't worry about it, it doesn't matter,' said Richard, walking from the shower with a towel wrapped around him. He dropped the towel and was standing naked with his back towards Paul as he got dressed.

Paul laughed. 'You did that on purpose, didn't you?'

'Yes,' said Richard. 'I want you to realise that there's nothing wrong with looking at someone's body, even if it is someone of the same sex.'

'I'm not so sure everybody would agree with you,' said Paul. 'It may be true for people of your age, but for me I was taught not to go around exposing myself like that. It was only after showers when we had games at school that people would walk around with nothing on. Even then the teacher would soon say, 'Put some clothes on, boy, where do you think you are?' and give you a clip round the ear. They laughed, but Paul said to Richard, 'It's true. Sex was very suppressed when I was a young teenager compared to now. If you tended to be a little introverted as I was you grew up knowing nothing. This led to curiosity which was usually satisfied by experimenting with other people of your own age, boys or girls. However, if deep down you thought "IT" was dirty, you held back. Quite wrong, obviously, but I suspect it still goes on now to some extent.' Paul looked at Richard suddenly realising what he had been saying. He blushed and didn't know what to say.

'Paul, I wish I'd known you when you were going through all of that torment. I could have helped,' said Richard.

36

'I do understand what you're saying. I think we all have our own ideas about sex, what is right, what is not; what is normal, what is not. From what I've heard and read about the Sixties free love hit the scene like a time bomb. For someone like you that must have been terrifying.'

'You're right in that.'

'All I'm saying is that we are friends. That means we can say anything to each other, and look at each other, with or without clothes. If that's what you feel like, it doesn't matter. Every relationship finds its own level and I think we both know where to stop,' said Richard. He walked up to Paul, put his arm round his shoulder and said, 'Come on, buddy, let's go to breakfast. All this talk of sex this early has made me hungry.'

They walked along the beach laughing. Paul felt on top of the world.

As it was their last day they decided to spend it by the pool. This way they could just laze around and not have to go too far for a drink or lunch. The pool looked very inviting, as usual, and the sunbeds were laid out in rows ready. Richard went to get a couple of towels from the pool attendant and they settled in for the day. Other guests soon started to take up their places by the pool ready for their dose of sun. Richard and Paul were both reading when Richard noticed the guy from the beach, the diver, walking around the other side of the pool. Richard nudged Paul and said, 'He looks just as good with his clothes on.'

Paul wondered what he was talking about until he saw where Richard's eyes were focused. He laughed and said, 'I wonder what he'd say if he knew that we saw him exercising his muscles yesterday.'

As the diver walked by he nodded and smiled at them. He went to the changing room. On the way back he stopped and introduced himself.

'I'm David, hello. I run the diving centre here, so if you want to go diving or want a lesson you only have to contact me. How long are you staying at the Island Lodge?' he asked.

'Unfortunately we are going back to Mahé tomorrow. Let us introduce ourselves – my name is Richard and this is Paul. We met on Praslin and decided to spend some time together on La Digue. Very enjoyable it's been too.'

'How do you do,' said Paul. 'It's a pity that we're going so soon. I'm afraid that we won't be able to take up your offer of a day's diving. I would need lessons anyway.'

'That's a shame, still, at least I can ask you to join me for a drink. It's not very busy at the moment, I don't have many clients,' said David.

'That sounds like a splendid idea to me. There's nothing that Paul and I like more than a nice cold beer. Right, Paul?' said Richard.

'Agreed,' said Paul. 'After you, David.'

They walked over to the bar and ordered three cold beers and asked Sotto if he could bring some crisps or nuts.

'Where are you from?' asked Richard. 'You seem to have a slight Australian accent.'

'I'm actually South African but I've lived in Australia for most of my life; if not there, here on the Islands,' said David.

'How long have you had the school at Island Lodge?' asked Richard.

'I came here at the beginning of the season; not that there is really a season. Diving goes on all year round,

38

even the locals go in for it. I have clients from Praslin and Mahé who come out every week,' said David.

'What do you do at night? Paul and I were saying the other day once the sun has gone down that's it. Nothing seems to open, no bars, no cinema.'

'That's true. If you haven't got a girlfriend or if you're not married there isn't much to do. We can get videos and we have television,' said David.

'Where do you live?' asked Richard.

'I have a flat in the village; it's only small but it suits me,' answered David.

'Do you live on your own?' said Richard.

'I do now. A friend of mine did share with me but he has gone back to Australia and so I have the place to myself,' replied David.

'Don't you find it a bit lonely living in a place like this? It's wonderful for a holiday but I'm not sure I could stand it all the time. Could you, Paul?' asked Richard.

'No, but we are town people, and I expect that makes us different as we like noise and other people around, except for breaks like this,' said Paul.

'It's not as bad as it seems. By working at the hotel I meet all the guests and sometimes the young ladies are quite pretty,' said David shyly.

'Have you ever been to London?' said Paul.

'Yes, I went to London before I went to Australia. It was very cold and I didn't see the sky once while I was there. It was cloudy all the time. I don't think I could live in London if it's like that all the time.'

'I know what you mean, but it's not always like that; if the weather is good it can be lovely.'

'I'd better go. I want to go diving myself this afternoon,' said David. 'I like to get some practice in if I can.'

'Yes, we know,' said Richard with a quick grin at Paul.

'Why don't you join us at the bar for a drink before dinner,' said Richard.

'Yes. I would like that. I'll see you later then,' said David, smiling as he went to collect his diving gear.

'He seems a nice bloke,' said Paul.

'Yes, but a screaming queen,' said Richard.

'What?'

'He's a gay.'

'How can you say that? Just because we saw him tossing himself off yesterday,' said Paul.

'No, I expect that you've done that before now – that doesn't make you gay. I see a lot of them in my business. I just know. You know what they say about actors,' laughed Richard. 'Anyway, enough of that.'

'Why did you ask him to join us for a drink tonight if that's the way you feel about him?' asked Paul.

'I don't feel anything about him. I'm sorry, I should have asked you first before I invited him to join us tonight.'

'I don't mind,' said Paul, 'but I wish you hadn't told me he was gay. You know me, I shall get all tongue-tied, and say all the wrong things. I might ask him how he enjoyed himself on the beach yesterday.'

'He might say he thought he was wonderful,' laughed Richard. 'Don't worry, I'll look after you, old buddy. Come on let's go for a walk along the beach.'

They walked off with Richard putting his arm around Paul's shoulders.

Later that evening, after Paul and Richard had met David in the bar, they decided to go back to Richard's chalet to play cards. Paul was not particularly good at card games. It was not something that you learnt unless you had brothers or sisters to teach you. After a while he excused himself and went to his own chalet. He said he would call Richard in the morning as they wanted to be on the early ferry to Praslin so that they could catch the flight to Mahé. They said their goodnights and David expressed his pleasure at having met him and wished him a safe journey.

At about four o'clock in the morning Paul awoke. As he listened to the noise that must have disturbed him he realised it was Richard and David saying goodnight. A bit late to be still playing cards, thought Paul, and went back to sleep.

The next morning riding the ox-cart Paul said to Richard, 'I heard David leave last night, about four, wasn't it?'

'Yes, I think so. I'm sorry we woke you, but you know how it is, a few more drinks, in fact, quite a few more drinks – the fridge is empty, and before you realise it it's nearly dawn.'

'That's OK. I know it must have been a bit hard for you with only me to talk to for the past week. David is more your age; I'm sure you found things to talk about,' said Paul.

'We did have a few things in common,' said Richard.

'Did he tell you about his time in Australia, where he'd been and what he'd been doing?'

'In fact, he'd been all over the place, and was thinking of staying there for good but he said he got home-sick for the islands. He came back three months ago.' Paul, why is it that you always think the best of people, he thought. 'No, it hasn't been difficult for me with only you to talk to. I've said before, we're mates. I like you, Paul and I like your company. I believe that we have had a great time. I'm beginning to look on you as one of my closest friends.'

'What about Chris? Surely as a business partner and an old school or university colleague he must have some claim on you as a friend?' said Paul.

'He certainly has got some claim on me, but I'm not sure it is as a friend.'

'What do you mean?'

'Oh nothing, but remember that most of the money for the business was put in by Chris and he's the one with the talent,' said Richard. 'Here we are, we should have walked and sent the bags by ox-cart. My bones ache everywhere.'

'Good idea, pity you didn't think of it earlier,' laughed Paul.

They boarded the boat and hoped this time it would not be as rough as the incoming journey.

Chapter 3

The journey from La Digue was without incident and the sea was as calm as anyone could have asked for. The flight to Mahé from Praslin was on time and they were able to pick up the luggage that they had left behind a week ago.

They were staying overnight at a hotel near the airport, as both Paul and Richard would be leaving the Seychelles the next day. Paul was going to Mauritius and Richard was going back to the UK.

They had breakfast and sat around waiting for the taxi to take them to the airport. Paul was the first to bring up the subject that had been taboo since it was first mentioned on La Digue.

'Richard, I really have enjoyed myself on this holiday and I'm convinced that you had a big part to play in that, perhaps more than you'll ever realise. I'm also aware that we are going back to the real world; where fifty-five-year-old pensioners do not go around with good-looking twenty-five year olds.'

Richard was laughing.

'What's the matter?' said Paul.

'I've never before thought of you as a pensioner. But

43

the way you put it it sounds so ridiculous. Believe me, Paul, when I say that I've never enjoyed myself so much either and I think you also played a big part in that. I know what you're going to say: can we meet in London? I still think you'll change your mind, but I'll give you a number that will reach me. If I'm not available just say Paul called. I'll ring you back. That is, of course, if you are going to give me a phone number to ring,' said Richard. He couldn't help grinning when he saw the look of pure happiness on Paul's face.

'Of course you can have a number and an address too,' said Paul. 'I promise I won't intrude on your life, but remember that we're mates and if you ever want anything just get in touch. If you want to get away from it all you can always stay. There's plenty of room. Bring your next girlfriend.'

'I really appreciate that, Paul. And I might take you up on the offer to stay, if things get really rough,' he added almost to himself.

The taxi driver arrived and they went to the airport. In the cab they exchanged phone numbers and Paul gave Richard his address and a brief explanation of how to get there. After that they sat quietly each with their own thoughts. When Richard's flight to London was called he and Paul shook hands and Richard pulled Paul towards him and hugged him. As he turned to go Paul saw tears in Richard's eyes.

Paul watched him board the plane and then watched the plane take off. He sat down and was immediately lost in his thoughts. Unlike him; he was usually checking out everybody at the airport for potential companions for the holiday. It didn't seem so important now. He had met Richard. He really did feel that what he had looked for over the years had at last turned up. He hoped so. Richard had so much going for him. He was without doubt a good-looking guy by anyone's standards. He knew that by the way David had looked at him, but it wasn't just that. He had good manners and seemed to be educated. He was certainly intelligent. It appeared that he was involved in a thriving business, although something still bothered Paul about that. Richard was often a bit secretive about his work. Uncharacteristic: Richard was the most open person he had ever met. He had only just got over the time when Richard had dropped the towel and had stood naked in the chalet – to get Paul used to the idea, he had said. Sometimes he was so streetwise it was frightening. After all, he was still only twenty-five.

Paul thought what he had been like at that age, not only him, but people that he had worked with who were twenty-five. They were not like Richard. They had no compassion.

The flight was called. Most of the other passengers had travelled from London. The flight was London – Dubai – Seychelles – Mauritius: quite a long haul. Paul's seat was on the outside of three. He sat down and fastened his seat-belt ready for take-off. The couple next to him were young but paid him no attention at all, he might just as well not have been there. The passengers opposite were older, he supposed about his age. The trouble was, having spent so much time with Richard, he did not feel his age. He decided he would pretend to be forty!

Paul had a book and was going to bury his nose in that except when the drinks and the food came round. He didn't feel like talking to anybody yet. They were up and away. The Captain was relaying over the intercom the speed and height they were travelling and what time they should arrive: fifteen-thirty. They arrived on time.

The trip from the airport to the hotel seemed to take

forever. He hadn't realised that Le Tousserok Hotel was on the opposite side of the island from the airport. They arrived at the hotel an hour and a half after leaving the airport. What a fabulous place. A wide reception area with lush settees for the guests, who were then greeted by the hotel staff, with, of course, the now almost mandatory fruit cocktail. One couple who were obviously honeymooners looked totally overwhelmed. The hotel was made up of small flats that were situated away from the main complex. Once given his key, Paul was shown to his chalet. This meant a walk across a bridge that passed the bar and was also a way to the restaurant. On the other side of the bridge signs with room numbers on were pointing everywhere. Paul thought even if he remembered his room number he doubted if he would ever find his room again. He must stay sober, he thought.

The next day he negotiated the paths from his room to the reception area without too much difficulty, and so decided to explore. As he wandered around he thought how he and Richard had prowled around the Island Lodge on La Digue. It had been fun. Experiences need to be shared, he thought again. It soon became apparent that this was a big hotel. The two islands that were a short ferry ride away, Île aux Cerfs and Îlot Mangenie, were where most people spent the day, although the beach outside his chalet looked very inviting too. Of the two islands, Île aux Cerfs was the one where all the entertainment was organised: water sports, volleyball, paragliding and boat trips. Îlot Mangenie was a quiet place with a lovely beach and a restaurant; no noise, not many people, paradise. Paul had found a closed-circuit television channel on the set in his room that told him all about the hotel, meal times and entertainment and so on. The entertainment in the bar every night looked promising. Cabarets with about fifteen to twenty people as singers and dancers for an hour or so. The swimming pool was under the restaurant and the disco was next to the pool. He found a games room which had a pool table and card tables on the first floor. A couple of days later he found that there was another swimming pool near the second restaurant by the beach.

I wish Richard was here, he thought, we could have had a terrific time together. Or would we? On the Seychelles we only had each other for company; here, the place was swarming with young people and a lot of unattached girls. Perhaps I wouldn't have seen Richard at all. Then how would I have felt? When they parted at the airport he had seemed genuine. Paul couldn't wait to see him again.

The two weeks that Paul spent on Mauritius were magic. Although the sun shone most of the time, it did rain also. After all, it was winter in this hemisphere. He went to one or other of the islands every day. Îlot Mangenie won most days. It was so beautiful and peaceful. He could swim and sunbathe at his leisure and then have a good lunch with some wine before returning to the hotel. In the evening nearly everybody met in the bar for a pre-dinner drink. The staff were friendly and went out of their way to make people feel welcome. Most of the English were honeymooners and preferred to stay on their own; those that weren't he spoke to and got on with quite well. Paul was surprised when it was time to pack to go home. Time had passed so quickly. He had loved every minute of his trip; it had been worth every penny. He was not looking forward to the seventeen-hour flight back, but he was looking forward to seeing his friends again and, of course, seeing Richard.

He had thought about Richard a lot since they had

parted. He knew a lot about the boy, but only from when they had met. He knew nothing about his background, except that he came from a village in Sussex. He never mentioned his parents or if he had brothers or sisters. He said that he had met Chris at university, that was all. He didn't say which university. Never any detail. He gave the impression that Paul would not get on with any of his friends. Yet he never spoke about them, never mentioned a name of one, not once. He gave Paul a telephone number where he could be contacted, but not an address of either the studio or his flat. Paul realised, the more he thought about it, that Richard had not told him a single thing about his life at home, what he did for fun or for business, except that he worked in a photographic studio. Did it matter? He liked Richard and wanted to recreate the relationship that they had had while on holiday. Maybe Richard had enjoyed it as much as Paul and was frightened that it would be ruined if they tried to contact each other in the harsh world of a big city. It was almost as if Richard had something to hide. That had come across even in the Seychelles. Yet they had been so open with each other. Paul remembered how he had told Richard of his lonely sex life and given the impression of how inexperienced he was in such matters. He must have been drunk, or at least had enough to loosen his tongue. Richard had been very understanding and had not made him feel a fool or like a dirty old man. He appeared to have a lot of knowledge of sexual activity, a lot more than was right for someone of his age. After that night they became closer. Richard relaxed more when he was with Paul; he didn't tense up if he touched him. He took to calling Paul 'dad'. He rather liked it. It was odd, but the answer Paul knew was in London.

After seventeen hours flying Paul got a cab from Gatwick. He couldn't face a coach and then a tube home. He wanted a good night's sleep. Unfortunately his body clock didn't agree with him. So he went to the supermarket to restock the cupboards.

In the post the next day Paul received a letter from Richard. He read it quickly, hoping it would say Richard would like them to meet up, but it didn't.

Dear Paul,

I know that you are home from your Indian trip as you liked to call it, and I wanted you to have some contact with me as soon as you got home. I can't say how much I enjoyed our bit of that trip. You are one of the nicest people I have ever met and I'll always look on you as a very special friend. Now that I am back in London and at work I know that what I felt on La Digue, about how us continuing to be mates here would not work, was true. I'd like to keep in touch though and if it's all right by you I will write now and again. We both lead different lives, Paul, and I don't think it would be fair on you for us to see each other again. I will miss you, dad. Take care of yourself. You will get hurt more than I could stand if we pretend that things are the same. They're not. I wish I had met you five or six years ago, things might have been different for both of us.

I'll always remember you and I'll write whenever possible.

Love Richard

Paul re-read the letter twice. He couldn't believe the tone of it. It sounded so hopeless. It sounded as though Richard did not have the joy for life that he had when he was with him. Paul knew he could not leave things like

49

this. He had to find out what made Richard write such a desperate letter. He was going into town in a couple of days for a drink with two ex-colleagues. He would wander around Bond Street to see if he could find any photographic studios.

Paul felt relieved that at least he had been right that there was something Richard was not saying about his work. He made up his mind to find out what it was. He was not going to stand by and watch someone he really cared for get hurt for any reason.

Two days after Paul had received the letter he was heading into town on the tube. Parking was so expensive and so difficult to find it was not worth taking the car. Besides, he was going to have a drink. He was also going to try to find out something about Richard's work place. He looked around the tube and wondered how he had put up with travelling into town every day for as long as he had. It was like a blank part of the day. Three hours, there and back, which normally you remembered nothing about at all. They had just pulled into Earl's Court station and the train was filling up. Paul looked around. Nobody of interest. He decided to get off at Green Park as he was a bit early and Alan was notorious for being late, not by much, but late. He turned left into Piccadilly and walked down to Piccadilly Circus. He turned to go towards Glasshouse Street when he was sure he saw Richard walking towards Leicester Square. Paul yelled but the boy did not look. Was it Richard? Perhaps he had been wrong; he had gone now anyway. Paul carried on to the pub. Alan turned up, late as usual, but they enjoyed the drinks that they had and had a few laughs. They talked about the business and all the latest gossip. They say time flies when you are having fun – it did that afternoon. And the drink flowed. When they did leave Paul was not sure whether to go to Bond Street or not. He decided to hell with it – he would come into town tomorrow and look for Richard.

As Paul was sitting on the tube travelling home his thoughts turned to the boy whom he had thought was Richard. I'm sure it was him, and yet he didn't even turn his head when I shouted. He must have heard me, everybody else did the way they looked at me. Paul suddenly remembered the phone number that Richard had given to him. When he got home he would ring the number and try to get hold of Richard, to confirm one way or another if it had been Richard in Piccadilly that afternoon.

The phone had been ringing for some moments. It stopped as someone finally answered it.

'Hello.'

'Could I speak to Richard Carter, please? I'm Paul Green.'

'Nobody here of that name,' said the voice that did not sound like the voice of someone who worked in a Bond Street photographer's.

'Are you sure? This is definitely the number I was given,' said Paul.

'Quite sure, but as I'm a bit new here I'll ask about a bit if you like and if I can, I'll tell him to ring you.'

'Thanks, that would be great. My name is Paul Green. Goodbye.'

'Cheers,' and silence. The phone had been put down.

Well, thought Paul, that was not what I would have expected from a studio with the reputation that Richard said they had. If he doesn't ring back I will certainly go into town tomorrow and find out what's going on.

However, Richard rang back.

51

Paul picked up the phone and was delighted to hear Richard's voice.

'Hi. Did you get my message?'

'Yes, did you get my letter?' said Richard. 'I thought I made it clear it would be best if we didn't see each other, and I don't want you phoning here. Believe me Paul, it's for the best.'

'You know that I can't accept that, and I won't. Your letter sounded so hopeless. We're friends and I'm going to see you whatever you say, my boy,' said Paul.

Richard was laughing down the phone 'OK. I'll meet you. Can I come out to your place?'

'You most certainly can, come for the weekend. Will you be driving?'

'No, my car's in the garage, but I've still got the instructions that you gave to me. I go to Hounslow East, don't I?'

'Yes and I'll meet you there, at about ten-thirty tomorrow.'

'I'm still not sure this is the right thing to do, Paul, but I'll see you.'

Richard hung up the phone.

Paul thought, what does that mean, not the right thing to do?

Richard put the phone down. How in God's name did I get into this mess, and how in God's name am I going to tell Paul? He had worried about Paul since returning from the Seychelles. He knew that he would want to get in touch, despite the letter.

'Dick, get yourself back into this studio, we've got work to do,' shouted a voice.

'OK, Chris, I'm coming,' answered Richard.

Richard was dressed casually in a pair of slacks and a

sports shirt. The weather was beginning to turn from summer to autumn and a jumper was something that most people were either wearing or carrying. Richard was no exception. While he was sitting on the tube his mind wandered back to the time that he and Paul had spent together. He realised that he had felt more relaxed with Paul than he had with anyone. They both liked each other, that was obvious. Richard liked the way Paul treated him. Paul treated him with respect, like an equal. He listened to what he had to say and appeared to be interested. Most people treated him like a commodity: something to buy or sell. Much as he was looking forward to seeing Paul again, he was still worried as to how the weekend would go. Richard had made up his mind that he was going to tell Paul everything, it was only fair. He knew that he would not be able to give Paul an edited edition of his life either. Once he had started he would not be able to stop. Richard suddenly came out of his reverie to discover that he had only one more stop to go. They were just pulling out of Osterly. The tube pulled into Hounslow East station and Richard could see Paul waiting for him on the platform. He could not help smiling when he saw him. Richard got off the train and shook hands formally with Paul.

'How are you, Paul? You look good – I see you finished up with a good tan.'

'Richard, it's good to see you too, and I see you haven't lost your tan either. I suppose you've been going to a health clinic for a couple of hours on a sun bed,' laughed Paul.

'Chance would be a fine thing,' grinned Richard. 'I've missed you, crazy isn't it?'

'No, I've missed you. Not least when I was staying on Mauritius. You would have loved it. I kept thinking of you, wondering what you were doing instead,' smiling like a parent who has just met his offspring for the first time in months.

'Come on,' said Paul. 'We can walk to my place from here, it's not far. How long are you staying? At least the weekend, I hope. Of course, you can stay as long as you like.'

'Slow down,' laughed Richard. 'This brings back memories of how excited you used to get when we were on La Digue. It also brings back memories of how easy we were in each other's company. I only hope it lasts.'

'What do you mean "I only hope it lasts"? Of course it will last, we're mates, remember. And because we are mates I want to know what's behind that letter, "I don't think it will be good for either of us to see each other again". What does that mean?' asked Paul.

'Paul, can we talk about this later?'

'Only if you promise to reveal all.'

Richard grinned. 'Yes I promise, only later.'

They had nearly arrived at Paul's house.

'It's very nice round here, Paul.'

'Yes, and it's handy. The shops are not far and there are parks within walking distance; also it's easy to get to London. Which is why I was happy to work in town for so long, I suppose,' said Paul. 'Well, here we are,' turning into the drive. He opened the front door and ushered Richard into the lounge.

'Very nice. I'm sure I shall be comfortable here, I think I will stay.'

Paul was grinning and fussing about like a mother hen. He went over to Richard and gave him a hug. 'It really is good to see you, son, I really missed having you about.'

Richard gave Paul a squeeze. 'I know, I missed you too.'

'Do you want a drink? A bit early I suppose, but who cares, or do you want to unpack and have a wash and brush up, as they say?'

'I would like to go to the bathroom, so I might as well unpack first.'

'In that case, I'll show you around.' They moved from the lounge into the hall.

'This is the dining room,' indicating a room on the left. 'This is the kitchen – I thought I would show you the kitchen so that you know where to come in the morning to make my breakfast.' Paul grinned. Richard grimaced.

'What is it, eggs and bacon or just toast?' asked Richard.

'I'll leave my order on the door tonight,' said Paul. 'Upstairs we have on the right my room, and on the left is your room. If there's anything that you need just ask. In front of you is my study or spare bedroom and the bathroom and toilet are behind you. I'll leave you to unpack. Join me in the lounge when you're ready. I'll make the drinks. Remember *mi casa es su casa* as they say in Mexican cowboy films. *Ciao.*'

Paul went downstairs to make the drinks. He thought Richard looked well. He was still as handsome as ever, it wasn't just the tropical setting that had turned him into a blushing schoolboy. It was the boy himself.

'Richard,' Paul called. 'Sorry, I forgot to say, there is space in the wardrobe for your clothes and the top two drawers are empty. If you need anything else, yell.'

'OK, Paul that's fine.' Richard had finished unpacking. He had one item left in his hand. It was a copy of a video he had made of his work. He still wasn't sure whether to show it to Paul or not.

Paul had made two margaritas. Richard saw them as he walked into the room.

'You don't miss a trick, do you?' he laughed. 'All we need now is the sun.'

'And David,' said Paul. 'Do you remember David?'

'Oh yes, I remember him,' said Richard.

'That's right, you thought he was gay, didn't you? He seemed all right to me,' said Paul. 'I quite liked him.'

'You like everybody, you'll get hurt one day. You're too trusting,' said Richard.

'So you told me in your letter. Don't think I've forgotten about it because you are here now. I still want to know what's going on,' said Paul.

'All right I promise. I'll tell you everything, but after dinner. I'm starving,' said Richard. 'Agreed?'

'Agreed,' said Paul.

Over dinner they reminisced about the fun that they had had on Praslin and the rough trip to La Digue, both laughing when they remembered how they had been looking at each other wondering which of them would be the first to throw up. Paul went to get the pictures he had taken and they looked at them together. Nothing but good memories. Richard asked how Paul had got on in Mauritius. Was that why he wanted to see him, to tell him that he had met another guy and that Richard was history?

Paul laughed.

'I had a great time and I'd like to go again, with you preferably.'

Paul left the table and sat on the settee. 'Everything I did I kept thinking, I bet Richard would like this. The two islands that were part of the hotel, one with all the activities such as paragliding and volleyball and so on, while the other one was like the beaches in the Seychelles – not another person to be seen if that was what you wanted. The sunbathing and swimming were marvellous.

I realised though that if you had been there I might not have seen as much of you as I would have liked.'

'Why do you say that?' asked Richard.

'Mauritius was not like the Seychelles, a lot of the guests were nearer to your age than mine and there were a lot of women. When we were on our own you had no choice.'

'You're crazy, do you know that? I still like you and I would still have liked you in Mauritius, other people would not have made any difference.' Richard had turned and was looking through the window out to the garden when he spoke, but nevertheless Paul thought he caught a slight choking sound in his voice.

'I'm really glad you said that, and I want to say something to you. Don't misunderstand what I'm going to say but give me a chance to explain. I think I love you. I'm not in love with you but I do love you like brothers can sometimes love each other, or like a father and son. I don't want to jump into bed with you, but I do want to hold you, to protect you and to have the warmth of your arms around me. I have never been in love with anybody, never been really close to anybody, and when I met you I knew that we would get on and could be friends. When I realised that you liked me too I was ecstatic. I know that I'm probably embarrassing you to hell and I'm sorry. But whatever you say, I hope that we can remain friends.'

Paul looked towards Richard for some sort of reaction. There was silence. Richard did not move. The silence was overwhelming. 'Richard, please say something,' begged Paul.

Richard turned to face Paul. Tears were streaming down his face. 'Why did you have to fall for me,' screamed Richard. 'Of all the nice blokes in the world

57

you pick me! It's not fair, I told you, Paul, that you would get hurt.'

'I don't understand,' said Paul.

'I'm not what you think. I'm a fucking rent-boy. I sell my arse, I suck cocks, anybody's cock if they pay me.' Sneeringly he added, 'And to supplement my income I make gay porno movies. I've even got a tape with me for you to watch.' Richard was by now sobbing uncontrollably.

Paul sat down. He was stunned. He did not know what to say.

'You see the nice young guy you thought you knew is just a whore,' cried Richard. 'I came here tonight to tell you the truth. I knew that it would be bound to get out once we were back in London, as it nearly did the other day when you called out to me in Piccadilly.' Richard fell into the armchair. 'And then you have to tell me that you love me. Paul, I love you too, but it can't work.'

Paul stood up slowly. He walked over to Richard and grabbed his arms. He pulled him to his feet and he hit him across the face. Hard. He hit him again and again.

'You stupid little fool, how could you let yourself get into such a degrading situation? Did you ever think about what you were doing? Performing acts of sexual gratification on men that you didn't know. Men who might be diseased, men who might harm you, even kill you. Why, for God's sake, what in hell made you do it? You're a good-looking boy who I am sure could have had anything you wanted. You chose to be a rent-boy. A perverted disgusting creature who will do anything for money. Does it turn you on to think some dirty old man is going to give you £20 to suck him off? You make me sick. Didn't you think about how other people would feel if they found out? Your parents, your friends, and I don't mean

this trash that you are now mixed up with. I could understand you being a homosexual, I suppose you are a homosexual, or do you have girlfriends? Girlfriends that you
can degrade as your clients do you. Have you any idea
of the risks that you've been taking. What about AIDS?
Have you been tested?'

'Yes. I'm HIV positive.'

'Oh, my God, Richard. What are we going to do? Get
up. Look at me. Promise me that you won't do anything
like this again,' said Paul.

Richard was a whimpering mess. His eyes were beginning to swell not only from crying but also from where
Paul had hit him. His nose was running – he looked
pathetic.

'I'm sorry Paul, you are the one person in the world
that I didn't want to hurt. I don't care about myself, I
know that I'm trash, but I didn't want to hurt you. I
couldn't help it. I was sixteen when I arrived in London.
No money and no job. Nowhere to live except with a
rent-boy, Chris,' said Richard.

'Promise me that you won't do this again,' said Paul.

'What else can I do,' screamed Richard. 'I'm a whore,
it's the only thing that I've done for the last ten years.'

Richard was sobbing uncontrollably, by now almost
incoherent.

'All right, take it easy,' said Paul. 'We can talk about it
in the morning.'

Richard looked at him. 'You mean you're not going to
throw me out?'

'What good would that do? Remember at the beginning
of this conversation I said that I loved you, which is why
I am so angry. I feel so helpless, but together we'll find a
way out and sort out a future for you, my boy,' said Paul.

Richard couldn't believe what he was hearing. Paul had

just torn him apart and made him feel disgusted with himself and now he was offering him solace and hope.

'I am grateful Paul. I don't know what else to say.'

'I think you've said enough for one night. I think we should go to bed and get a good night's sleep,' said Paul.

They went upstairs. Paul looked at Richard and put his arm round his shoulders as he had done on holiday. He led him into his room.

'I think we both need someone to hold tonight, don't you?' They went to bed.

Chapter 4

Richard Carter, born seventh November 1967. His parents owned a farm in the village of Frogham in Sussex. A small place that most people could never find, and they had never heard of it anyway. The nearest big town was Haywards Heath about twenty-five miles away.

Richard grew up learning to love the country and country life. As a small child he had lots of fun in the fields. He could wander down to the river, into the woods, go where he liked. Nobody ever told him 'don't do that' or 'leave that alone', or 'come here, stay in the house'.

He went to the village school when he was five years old. The school, like the village, was small, only about a hundred and fifty pupils, all between five and eleven. He liked school and picked things up easily. He did well, which pleased his parents. Once a month his mother would take him shopping. This meant going into Haywards Heath. Richard loved it. It was so much more exciting than school, or playing in the woods. The town had lots of people all rushing around and buses and cars racing up and down the roads. It was a different world.

When he reached the age of eleven his parents decided

to send him to a private school. He learnt that he was to go to Barnbury, about ten miles away, and that he was to be a boarder during the week and come home at the weekends. Richard was not at all sure that he liked the idea, but he wasn't asked. He had an aptitude for school work and his parents wanted the best for him, trying to give him every encouragement. After all, he was their only child.

On the appointed day Richard and his mother set forth to Barnbury. Richard hated it. It wasn't the work or the teachers – it was the older boys. Some of them were bullies and they would hit him for no reason and make him fetch and carry for them. Richard had spent most of his life on his own, except when he was at school and then everybody was supervised; he didn't know how to handle bullying. On domestic night, when the dormitory had to be cleaned, he was always made to do more than his fair share, and always made to clean the lavatory. A farmer's boy should be used to cleaning up shit, he was told. Richard tried to fight back, but he didn't get a lot of support. After all, if he was being bashed about the other boys were being left alone, and they liked it that way. This made Richard a loner, but he didn't mind. He had always been on his own on the farm.

By the time Richard had reached the third year life was beginning to improve. The bullies had left and he began to find some friends. He was happy. He was also growing up. Things were starting to happen to his body. He understood what was going on from biology lessons, and he had heard the older boys talk at night. So it was no surprise to him when he played with himself that a thick creamy sort of liquid shot from his prick. Nevertheless, he didn't tell anybody.

Richard at fifteen had grown into a very good-looking

boy. His dark eyes and jet black hair, his broad smile and his pleasant personality all helped to make him popular. When he went home at weekends the girls in the village would giggle as he passed.

The ladies in the village would say to his mother, 'Your Richard will break a few hearts before long, Mary Carter'. Deep down Mary was very proud to think that her son had all of the girls after him. Maybe she would have grandchildren sooner than she had anticipated.

Saturday night was the big night in the village. The village hall, used for the Women's Institute, scouts and jumble sales, was turned into a dance hall. Lights were put up and a band was hired for the evening. The entire village dressed up and attended the Saturday Night Dance. Richard and the other teenagers were no exception; what else was there to do? Watch television or go into Haywards Heath, and for that you needed transport.

Just after his fifteenth birthday Richard was at the dance, as usual on Saturday, when Patsy Fisher, whose father worked on a neighbouring farm, came up to him and asked him to dance. Richard was surprised. He knew Patsy, he knew everybody in the village, but he had never spoken to her much. They bounced around on the dance floor and when the music finished Richard thought, thank God, and having said thank you to Patsy, started to walk away. Patsy held on to his arm.

'Shall we go outside for a while?' she said.

'Are you mad? It's the middle of December. It's freezing out there,' said Richard.

'Don't be such a baby, come on,' said Patsy.

Anything for a quiet life, thought Richard and went with her. They went round to the back of the hall and stopped. Patsy made a lunge for Richard and kissed him. Richard was more surprised than anything. He had never thought that he might have one of the girls from the village as a girlfriend. She kissed him again. It was all right but it didn't make him feel any different.

'Don't you like me?' asked Patsy, pushing herself towards him so that he could feel her breasts against his chest.

'Of course I like you,' said Richard.

'Well, I don't mind,' said Patsy.

'Don't mind what?' asked Richard.

'I don't mind if you touch me. You're so good looking, Richard Carter, that you make my legs go weak,' said Patsy.

She was deliberately rubbing her breasts against Richard and she had put her leg between his. Richard could feel he was getting a hard on. Oh my God, he thought, she's bound to feel it. She did. Before Richard knew what was happening Patsy had unzipped his flies and had her hand inside his trousers.

He put his hand onto her breast and started to unbutton her blouse. He slipped his hand inside and came across her bra. He paused, not knowing what to do. He tried to get his fingers underneath, without too much success. He tried to get his hand around the back of her so that he might undo the wretched garment. At last he managed it and he was able to feel her breast with his bare hand.

'Ooh,' cried Patsy. Richard had shot his load into her hand. He couldn't help it. She had been rubbing his cock through his underpants, but she got her fingers inside and touched his flesh. That was that.

They pulled apart and after cleaning up and dressing properly they went back to the dance. Patsy went to her friends and Richard went to Ken.

The next week back at school Richard thought a lot about his fumblings with Patsy. He decided that what made him excited was her touching him, not him touching her. Having come to that decision, he thought no more about it and continued to relieve himself nightly as usual until the Christmas holidays arrived.

He was not looking forward to the holidays with his parents. He seemed to have more arguments with his father every weekend. Always about something silly. He knew that there would be another row when he told his parents that he was going to a disco in Haywards Heath on Christmas Eve. Sure enough, there was. The place was licensed. Frank Carter refused to allow him to go to a place that was licensed when he was only fifteen. 'How did you think you were going to get home? You needn't think that I am going to pick you up,' yelled Frank. Richard explained that Ken's brother had a car and he was taking them and would also bring them back. It didn't work. Frank Carter would not believe that Ken's brother was going to stay sober all night in order to bring a couple of kids home from a disco. He was more likely to find himself a girl and stay with her the night, 'and he wouldn't want you two watching,' said Richard's father.

Richard went anyway although he knew that he would get a thumping from his father when he got home, even if it was Christmas Day.

Things got worse after that. Richard and his father could not agree on one simple thing. His mother smothered him. At school he felt frustrated, it was all too easy, he needed a challenge. His brain needed a challenge. He made up his mind in that term that as soon as he was sixteen he was going to leave and get himself a job and earn some money. He hated the farm and the country.

Richard left home at sixteen and a half years old. Neither his mother nor his father knew that he had gone until the next day. They thought he would be back before long.

Richard had some money, but not much. He had stolen some from his mother; enough for a train ticket to London, Victoria. He hadn't got the faintest idea what he was going to do when he got there, but he didn't care. He would be free, out of the straitjacket that he felt he had been forced into for the past couple of years.

He arrived in London in April 1983. He looked around, aware that he must be standing out like a sore thumb. Everyone seemed to have somewhere to go – he couldn't make up his mind which exit of the station he should use. He realised that he was hungry and could do with something to drink. He went to the burger bar that was nearby and ordered some food and a drink. As he was eating a boy who was perhaps two or three years older started to talk to him.

'Hi, just got in?' he asked.

'Yes,' said Richard.

'Have you got anywhere to stay, because you realise that you can't stay here. The trade would kill to get to you,' said the boy.

'What do you mean?' asked Richard.

'With your good looks and at your age you'll have every queer in the area after you. You do know what queer means, don't you?' asked the boy.

'Of course I do. I'll just tell them to piss off,' said Richard.

'Fat lot of good that will do. Besides if you start yelling the police will be here before you know it. They'll put you on the first train home. Is that what you want?'

'No,' said Richard. 'What do you suggest?'

'We are posh, aren't we? What do you suggest? I suggest that you come with me, at least for tonight, you can sleep on the settee. That is, if you want to,' offered the boy.

'Yes, thank you. My name is Richard. What do I call you?'

'Chris.' They shook hands.

They went back to a one-room flat off the Earl's Court Road. That was home for Chris. Richard looked around. It wasn't much, but it was more than he had at the moment.

'What do you do for a living?' asked Richard.

'I'm a rent-boy,' said Chris. 'No use beating about the bush, you might as well know straight away. You'd soon find out.'

Richard looked at him in amazement. He had heard of that sort of thing, but supposed that he had never really believed it.

'Do you make a lot of money doing it?' said Richard. He couldn't think of anything else to say.

'Yes. You can if you have the looks that the punters go for. Have you got any plans?' asked Chris, looking at Richard as if he were putting a value on a racehorse.

'No, not really. I just had a row and walked out,' said Richard.

'Do you want to go back, because if you do I'll give you the money for your fare,' said Chris.

'Why would you do that when you hardly know me?' asked Richard.

'I've seen what can happen to kids your age coming to London without money or contacts,' said Chris.

'Thanks anyway, but I think I'll stay for a while,' said Richard.

'You can stick around with me and I'll show you how to make a few quid,' said Chris.

Richard looked at him to make sure that he understood

what Chris was offering. 'I don't know. I've never done anything like that before,' he said.

'Don't tell me you've never had a wank before, that's all a lot of them want. Some want a blow job, but you soon get used to that. If you don't like the look of them, put the price up. Don't be too fussy, the word soon gets round. Look, you don't have to sleep on the settee tonight. Sleep in my bed and maybe I'll give you a few free lessons,' said Chris, thinking to himself, I'd really like to break this one in myself. Still, slowly does it. Not all on the first night.

That was how it all started. Richard was soon touring the main-line stations to pick up trade. He was very successful. He tried to get a proper job, but he soon got bored with them. He was so young that he always got the jobs that were the most monotonous. Never any responsibility, never a challenge to his mind. Like school, he thought. He was often out late cruising Piccadilly and would sometimes take men back to his flat until the small hours. Consequently he was tired and looked awful the next morning. He was late for work. Jobs did not last too long. He saved as much as he could, telling himself that he would be off to start afresh as soon as he had enough money. Always as soon as he had enough money. At first, he hated what he was doing. The first time he was fucked he was terrified, but he became hard and bitter. He got used to it. He was twenty now and had grown into a very handsome man. And he knew it, and how to use it. He would smile at a potential customer and they were like putty in his hands, but not for long.

Richard had left Chris's flat after a few months and was now buying a flat of his own off the King's Road. Chris had bought a studio and was taking photographs for a living, mostly of men for gay magazines. He had some legitimate work too; models and actors always wanted new pictures. The studio was in Bond Street, a good address. Richard had not seen Chris for some time. They had both gone their separate ways when Chris started up the studio. So it was quite a surprise to Richard when he answered a knock at his front door to see Chris standing there.

'Chris,' said Richard. 'Nice to see you. Come in. What are you doing here after all this time?'

'Is it really that long? I came because we're old friends and I hadn't seen you for a while,' said Chris.

Richard laughed. 'Bullshit, you must have an ulterior motive, so come on, get on with it. I'll get some beer so you can have time to think about how to dress it up.'

'True, so I'll come right to the point. I've been making some enquiries into porn movies, and I can tell you it's big money. It's the fastest growing industry this country has got. I have been to Germany and Holland – they are the main distribution points – and they'll pay a fortune for the right sort of film. I've decided to go for it. I've managed to pick up a camera or two and some other bits and pieces, and I've had the studio refurbished so that I've got a private studio where I can film what I like and without interruptions. I'll also be able to carry on with my legitimate work. What I need now is people, which is why I'm here. I thought to myself, who do I know that has the good looks and the other qualifications to be a good porno star? I thought, Richard Carter. The very one,' said Chris with a laugh.

'I don't know, Chris. You know that I'm no good with women, I don't think I could do it for you.'

'Who said anything about women, I'm talking about a gay movie. That's where the money is,' said Chris.

'What would I have to do?' asked Richard.

'First you would have to change your name; Richard Carter doesn't sound right for a skin flick. How about the shortened version of Richard; Dick. Yes Dick, but Dick what? Dick Hard – that would look great on the credits,' said Chris.

Richard was roaring with laughter. 'OK. What the hell, from now on I'm Dick Hard, porno star.'

A couple of weeks later he went to the studio to shoot his first movie. He was a bundle of nerves, ridiculous really. When he arrived he was told by the receptionist to take a seat. Two other guys were waiting. He knew one of them; he worked the same areas as Richard. The other was a stranger to him. He was blond and tall, about six foot three inches, and had the sort of body that showed that he worked out regularly. They each looked at the other, probably wondering if the other two knew what was going on.

Chris arrived and showed them into the studio where they would be filming. He introduced everybody and then said they should get started.

At first it was awful. They were all so self-conscious, you would have thought that they had never taken their trousers off before. The cameras made them nervous. When Chris stopped filming and would say, 'Can we do that again? I didn't have a good angle,' it was almost impossible. After a while they relaxed with each other and it started to go very well. Richard proved to be the best. Apart from being the best looking, he had an affinity with Chris and seemed to know exactly what he wanted and so was always in the right position. Richard knew what was expected of him and when he was at a climax point he made sure that Chris was aware of it too for the sake of the camera.

Richard's bank balance grew. He discovered the Seychelles. A paradise where he could be Richard Carter again and meet ordinary people who liked him as a respected businessman. He met Paul Green.

Richard put down the phone. How in God's name did I get into this mess, and how in God's name am I going to tell Paul? He had worried about Paul since returning from the Seychelles. He knew that he would want to get in touch, despite the letter.

'Dick, get yourself back into this studio, we've got work to do,' shouted a voice.

'OK, Chris. I'm coming,' answered Richard.

Chapter 5

Paul was looking at the boy lying next to him. His beautiful face, his broad shoulders, his lean torso leading to his slim waist, his rounded buttocks and his strong muscular legs. The boy was a modern-day Adonis, and he had fallen in love with him. He was crazy and he knew it. He also knew this must be a fantasy. This was not part of his real life. He wondered what he was going to say to Richard. The startling revelations that he had made last night had left Paul dumbfounded. He had grown very close to Richard on holiday and he had thought that he knew him quite well. He still could not believe it – a rent-boy and a porno film star. It just wasn't the Richard he had known in the Seychelles. Why did he say that he loved him? He had fallen for other boys in the past and had never said a word to anyone. He had got over it and nobody had been any the wiser, and, more importantly, nobody had been hurt. This was going to be different. He had told Richard that he loved him; two people were already hurting almost more than either of them could bear. Richard would never have expounded on his life if he hadn't been pushed. If only he had taken notice of his letter instead of playing detective. Selfish bastard, he thought, that would have got you off the hook, but what about Richard, where would that have left him? Exactly where he was, making porn films or selling himself on the streets. God, he still couldn't believe it.

Paul was stroking Richard's hair. The poor kid was shattered last night, he shouldn't be left on his own. He could stay here, we'll see when he wakes up how he feels about that.

Paul showered and started to make breakfast. It was a wonderful day – sunny, with an icy freshness in the air. Not uncommon at this time of the year. Perhaps they could go for a walk. Richmond Park was not too far and they would be able to talk in private and get some exercise.

'Good morning,' said Richard quietly as he entered the breakfast room. 'First, I want to say that I'm sorry for all of the pain and embarrassment that I've caused you. The one person in the world that I didn't want to hurt, ever. I'm sorry. I know that you said we could talk this morning, but if you've changed your mind I understand and I'll leave straight away. Please Paul, try to remember me as you knew me on La Digue, not as a filthy pervert who has sex with any man who will pay him or who'll perform in front of a camera. I couldn't stand that.'

'I don't want you to go, Richard. I want to understand. I'm normally a good judge of character and I don't see why I should be so wrong about you. I want you to explain to me how you got into your situation and why you didn't get out when you must have realised exactly what you were becoming – a whore. I've been gay all of my life and I've never given in to the temptation to sleep with another man once. I've always kept my feelings to myself and acted out my fantasies on my own. I'm not saying I'm typical – I know that I'm not, but then, nor are you. You gave me no hint that you were gay when we were on holiday. How did you manage that, particularly as you must have known that I was gay and that you were driving me to distraction? I don't understand,' said Paul.

'I think that you and I have shocked each other quite a bit over this weekend. Until last night I had no idea that you were gay. I thought that you were a little bit naive, but people like you who are single and devote so much time to their careers often are. I was even trying to protect you from the likes of David. Remember him? We watched him masturbating on the beach. I thought you were shocked, not excited. When you saw me naked a few times I thought you were a little embarrassed. It never occurred to me that you might be gay and fancied me. I don't know why, I suppose that I've become so hard that I don't recognise the signs in an ordinary homosexual. I see the street boys and their customers and the porn stars. The gays without any subtlety or sensitivity. I had forgotten that plenty of gay men never have more than two or three partners, some, none at all, while others have one partner for life. I liked you from the first time we met at the airport, or rather noticed each other. I should have realised then. I knew that the age difference would be about thirty years but that didn't matter. It might have been just what I was looking for. I had recently been diagnosed HIV positive, I had no one to turn to, I was scared. In my line of work you don't get much sympathy. I ran away to the Seychelles and met a guy who liked me for myself. I didn't know that it was the body you were after, I thought it was the mind,' grinned Richard. 'I suppose a shrink would say I was looking for a father figure. I know all I wanted to be was the same as everyone else, just for once.'

'Well, at least I've given you something to smile about,' said Paul.

'I remember when we met at the Meridian Hotel, I thought that here was a guy who was more alone than I was. Why shouldn't we get together and enjoy ourselves? It would help me with my problems and maybe it would help you to forget, if there was something to forget. I never dreamt that it would turn out like this. I was convinced that when we got back to London that would be that. It was only when we were on La Digue and you talked about meeting after you got back from Mauritius I realised it wasn't going to be so easy. My fantasy was turning into reality,' said Richard.

'I still don't understand how you became a rent-boy in the first place,' said Paul.

Richard told the entire story from when and why he had left home at sixteen and a half, to how Chris had asked him to star in his films. Richard didn't leave out any detail. Some of the things he said made Paul gasp and display emotions of disgust. Richard knew that he had to tell it; it was like a cleansing process. He tried to explain to Paul how at first he couldn't see anything wrong with being a rent-boy. He had enjoyed many hours with Ken, his friend from home, as they tossed each other off. What was the big deal? He knew that Ken had done it with other boys too. It was easy money. It was more than he could get from a straight job. He was seventeen, all the work going was of the most monotonous type – filing in an office, sweeping up in a shop, washing up in a restaurant. He had a brain, he needed a challenge. He ended up back on the streets. He didn't care any more. He would do anything for money. When Chris asked him to join the firm he did, without hesitation. It was there that he became HIV positive. He had spoken aloud things that he had never said to another living person. He had told Paul all about his life and it had drained the blood from his face; he was a deathly white. He could not look at Paul.

'I can understand how you got into all of this and I think I can understand why you haven't got out of it. However, I think you have got to make up your mind now as to what you're going to do. Carry on as you are and be dead, after infecting others, in a couple of years, or change your life style. Nobody can guarantee you a long life, but I can guarantee you a happy one here with me. Don't say anything yet, before you do I would like to see your video. I can't pretend that I want to see it out of curiosity, I want to look at you. If you say no, fair enough,' said Paul.

'You know more about me than anybody in the world, so, yes, you can see it, but not while I'm in the room. That I couldn't take. I think you'll find it an education. It's called porn because that's what the establishment calls it. It's not as bad as some blue movies that I've seen. It's not violent and in some places it's quite tender and loving, but fake. The love scenes in any film are not real, these are just more explicit.

'I can't believe I heard you right, but did you say I could stay with you?' said Richard.

'Yes. I meant what I said last night. I love you Richard, and I'll do all that I can to help you through this major crisis in your life. We can talk about it later, but we need to make plans for your future,' said Paul. 'I thought we might go for a walk in Richmond Park, it's nice there. First, though, I'm going to the pictures. See you later.'

Paul walked into the lounge with a video tape of a man he loved, not knowing quite what to expect.

He watched the video. He could not believe what he was seeing. Paul had never even seen a straight blue movie, let alone anything as explicit as this. The full-frontal nakedness of the actors in an aroused state had a startling effect on Paul. He watched, his eyes never leaving the screen, as the sex acts took place: oral sex, anal sex, masturbation and close-up shots of orgasms. Paul was highly excited. He was hot and shaking. The film came to an end and Paul calmed down. He started to think about what he had seen. He could understand why Richard was a star. He was a natural in front of the camera, and the camera liked him. His good looks seemed to be enhanced on screen and his smile was enough to make even the most critical viewer succumb to his charms. Paul had also noticed that what Richard had said was true. The movie wasn't violent, in parts it was very tender. When Richard was kissing the other actor and caressing his body, it appeared to be a loving gesture rather than one of lust. The collapse into each other's arms after intercourse showed satisfaction and gratification by both lovers, which is what they were in the film. Paul watched it again.

'You're quite a stud, aren't you,' smiled Paul when he returned the tape to Richard.

Richard was embarrassed and turned his eyes from Paul.

'I'm sorry, I was only trying to make light of something that's difficult for both of us,' said Paul.

'It's knowing that you know. The innocence of our holiday has gone, hasn't it?'

Paul could see that Richard was very unhappy knowing that Paul had seen the tape. Richard wanted things to be as they were two months ago. 'I don't think either of us can pretend that things are the same. They're not. We've both been more honest with each other than either of us has been with anyone else. Inevitably that meant exposing a more unsavoury side of our nature. I believe that through that honesty the strength of our relationship will grow, and we'll be friends for a long time to come. Come here,' said Paul.

Richard moved nearer to Paul. Paul put his arms around him, hugged him and kissed him lightly on the face.

'Let's go for that walk we were talking about. I think I've regained my strength after watching that video. Twice,' grinned Paul.

'You dirty old man,' laughed Richard.

They drove to Richmond Park but left the car by the restaurant and walked towards the ponds.

'We need to talk about the future,' said Paul. 'There are a lot of loose ends to sort out. What, for example, are you going to do now? You'll have to get a job of some sort. How do you think Chris will react to you not working for him? I take it you've decided to give up your old life?'

'Yes, of course I have. But as for the rest of it, I don't know. Remember, I was just a stupid kid of sixteen when I left home and all I've known since is the streets. It doesn't exactly make good reading on a CV. I'm a bit worried about Chris and what he will say – as you said, I'm a natural. God, what an epithet. He can make big money from what I do. Correction – from what I used to do,' said Richard.

'Why are you worried about Chris? I thought you said he was a friend?'

'He is, but, oh, I don't know. If he hasn't got another actor to take my place, and you don't usually pick them up through auditions out of drama school, he might insist that I carry on, or else,' said Richard, thinking much more than he was saying.

'Do you mean Chris could coerce you into making another film for him?' asked Paul.

'I don't think he would have me beaten up or anything like that, but when you're working in the business that he is in you undoubtedly meet some criminal types. It's not beyond the realms of possibility that Chris could have my flat wrecked. Don't forget also I'm a prime target for blackmail, particularly if I did get a straight job and was making a go of it,' said Richard. 'I'm just telling you this because I want you to know what you're taking on by harbouring me. The best thing I can do is to go to see Chris and put it to him straight. I would like to get any copies of any tapes that he has in which I feature. I don't know if that's possible; I expect he would want a few hundred pounds for them, and I haven't got that sort of money.'

'Don't worry about the money. I'll lend it to you and you can pay me back whenever you can. How many films are we talking about?' asked Paul.

'Three, including the one you've seen. Chris always said to me that all the films he made were distributed in Amsterdam and Hamburg. None of them were sold to dealers in London. I know that they could always be smuggled into this country, but I've never heard of any and as the last one was made, or, at least, distributed two years ago, maybe they're old hat and won't suddenly appear over here. God, I hope so,' said Richard.

'Did you say that it was two years ago that the last film you made was distributed?' asked Paul.

'Yes, about that.'

'What have you been doing since? How have you lived?' asked Paul.

'I've been back to hustling again. Not on the streets, a bit more up-market. Chris has been acting as my pimp, if you like, he makes dates for me and I visit the client, usually at his home. Sometimes, if they are married or for some reason can't do that, they come to my place. It's arranged for me to stay the night occasionally, but normally it's only for an hour. The money I can make is a lot more than working the stations or hanging around the meatrack, as it's known. I would probably have only one or two clients a night. Whereas at ten to fifteen pounds on the streets I would expect to have ten or more blokes a night.' Richard hated talking like this to Paul and forced himself to imagine that he was explaining about someone else's life.

'Oh, I see,' said Paul feeling somewhat embarrassed. 'Right, I think the first move is for you to see Chris and tell him the situation. Offer him money for the master tapes of those that you want. Tell him that you've sold your flat to help pay for them. Whether you tell him you've moved in with me is up to you. In the meantime I'm going to get in touch with an old friend of mine who has a production studio, in fact, it's now one of the biggest independent production houses in London. I've been thinking since I have seen you in front of the camera, I think you should use your assets,' said Paul.

'That's what I have been doing for the last few years,' grinned Richard.

'I was thinking that you could keep your clothes on this time,' smiled Paul. 'You really have got a dirty mind.'

'It's taken years of practice,' said Richard, smirking.

'I'm serious,' said Paul. 'Why don't you try to get into acting school? You're a very handsome young man and you do look good on screen. I don't know how much acting was required in what you were doing, but at least you have been in front of a camera. What do you think?'

'It's not something I'd ever thought about, legitimate acting. I suppose I could do it. I know I would certainly like to try. Do you think your friend will be able to help?' said Richard.

'I think John will be able to put us on the right road, maybe even open a few doors. I'll go to see him tomorrow when you're seeing Chris,' said Paul.

Paul felt a lot happier now that something specific had come out of the day. He was beginning to wonder if he had made the right decision in talking Richard into going straight. After all, he had made good money for the last five or six years.

'What about the HIV thing, Richard? Is it certain that you're infected? Didn't I read somewhere that a new drug had been developed to slow down HIV turning into AIDS? What have you been told?' asked Paul.

'What I've been told is more or less what you can read in the papers. I've always been to the clinic to make sure that I'm clean and the last time I was told that I was positive. I know that it's fatal and that there is not a known cure yet. Everybody dies. Some take a lot longer than others. Some people take years to develop AIDS and even then don't become ill immediately. I don't know. I was given some leaflets about counselling, but at the time I didn't want to know. In denial, I think it's called. Now I think it's time that I did get some advice. I'm almost as much in the dark as you,' said Richard.

'Who else knows that you are HIV positive?' asked Paul.

'Nobody, except you.'

'I think it would be a good idea to tell Chris. Particularly if he's being difficult. After all he's not going to want to put all of his stars at risk,' said Paul.

'I hope you don't mean that as it sounds,' said Richard. 'It makes me sound as though I would sleep with anybody and, knowing that I'm infected, not tell them.'

Paul blushed. 'Yes I'm sorry that is how it sounded. It's not what I meant. What I meant to say was that if Chris knows that you won't be able to perform, act for him as you have done in the past, he may be only too happy to let you go,' said Paul.

'Yes, I see what you mean,' said Richard. He was beginning to get some colour back in his cheeks and the sparkle in his eye. He smiled that devastating smile at Paul. Paul thought, if you have the effect on a quarter of the audience that you have on me you're going to be a star.

'I'm getting hungry. Let's go to the pub down by the river,' said Paul.

'Good idea. I'm starved too. Last one to the bar buys the drinks,' announced Richard as he raced off with all the exuberance of youth.

Paul watched Richard, amazed at the fortitude of the young. Paul was worried about the tapes and Chris's reaction when he found out that his prime asset was going to quit. Richard still thought of Chris as a friend and, although he had told Paul about the possibility of his flat being wrecked, he really didn't think it was likely.

'I thought margaritas were a bit over the top at lunchtime so I've ordered you a pint of bitter,' grinned Richard.

'That's fine. What are you going to have to eat? I think I'll have a plate of pie,' said Paul.

'Thanks. I'll have a ploughman's, if that's OK,' said Richard.

'Of course,' said Paul thinking, he'll survive. He's a born survivor. He must be to have lived the life he's led for the last ten years and still to have retained some charm and manners; rare enough in the young these days. Richard arrived at the table with the two beers and set them down. He sat down himself and looked directly into Paul's eyes.

'Paul, you're not saying all of this about acting and my moving in with you just to cheer me up, are you? I couldn't bear that. Not after last night. When you hit me, something within me snapped. It made me look at myself and I was disgusted at what I saw. For the first time I saw myself as others see me. I'm so ashamed. I could have easily put my head in the gas oven, but I noticed that you were electric,' smiled Richard.

Although he had made a joke of it, Paul knew that he had been in the frame of mind to kill himself last night. He knew that if he had not had the love and warmth that Paul had given him in bed, Richard may not have been there then.

'I would never be so cruel,' said Paul. 'I meant every word and tomorrow you are going to see Chris and I am going to see John. It's the start of a new life. Dick Hard is dead. Long live Richard Carter.'

'I'll drink to that,' said Richard.

'There's one more thing,' said Paul. 'Don't you think that you should contact your parents, just to let them know that you are all right?'

'No, I did ring Ken once when I was feeling down, and it seemed as though my parents made little effort to find me or to find out where I'd gone. The word around the village was that as far as they were concerned "if he wants to go, let him". Can you imagine? I was sixteen and a half! Anyway, I thought you wanted to be my dad; I much prefer you,' laughed Richard.

'Fair enough,' said Paul. 'After lunch you had better go

to your flat and pack your clothes. The rest of your stuff can be put into store for the time being.'

'I haven't got a lot really. My music centre and CDs, a tele, and a few books. The furniture I think I'll try to sell with the flat. If I can't I'll sell it separately, I don't want to store it for what could be some months,' said Richard. 'I'll do that tomorrow. Let's go home.'

'Yes, it's getting a bit dark and cold,' said Paul.

They drove in silence, both men embroiled in their own thoughts.

After they had arrived at the house and settled in the lounge Richard said, 'Paul, you know more than anybody about me, and I know very little about you, come on, tell me all of your dark secrets.'

Paul laughed.'There's not a lot to tell, and you know most of it. You know that I'm fifty-five, pushing fifty-six, that I have just taken redundancy and retirement, and that I'm gay and always have been. I've never had a boyfriend or a lover, I just couldn't commit myself to that life style. It wouldn't be true to say that I have never wanted a lover because I have. Some guys I met when I was younger, your age, nearly sent me out of my mind. Somehow I always stayed in control. I didn't get married, although everybody thought I would, at least until I was about forty, I think they gave up after that. I worked in the tv industry, which I loved, and so I put my heart and soul into it. I have always liked travel and when I went on holiday I would fantasise about meeting someone with whom I could spend the holiday. I never did until I met you.'

'It might have been better if you hadn't met me,' said Richard.

'I'll ignore that. You were exactly what I had been dreaming about, a good-looking hunk of twenty-five who could hold an intelligent conversation, and, when he smiled at me, made me go weak at the knees,' said Paul.

'And I didn't realise,' said Richard shaking his head.

'I had thoughts and did things that I hadn't done for years because of you. You made me feel younger and I needed you as much as it now seems that you needed me. I had just taken redundancy and retirement, I was lonely. I began to wonder if I'd done the right thing. What was I going to do with the rest of my life?'

'Then I turned up and gave you more problems than you could cope with,' said Richard.

'Ain't that the truth,' said Paul laughing. 'That's about it.'

'Don't you have any family?' asked Richard.

'No. Some cousins somewhere, but after both of my parents had died and one or two of the aunts and uncles that we were close to, I lost touch. We still exchange Christmas cards, but that's about all,' said Paul.

'We are a pair of idiots really, aren't we?' said Richard. 'We both seem to have taken extreme paths in our lives, you being cold and aloof because you were frightened of having a relationship and me sleeping with half of London because I couldn't find love.'

Richard got up and moved over to sit next to Paul, he put his arm around his shoulder.

'Paul, I will never put you at risk of being infected with the dreaded disease, but a hug and a kiss and a cuddle now and again is OK, isn't it?'

'Of course it is, stupid,' said Paul, roughing up Richard's hair.

Richard grinned and looked like a puppy rewarded for retrieving a ball.

'I did mean it when I said that you looked good in front of the camera, and I didn't mean only with your clothes off either. If you have any talent at all, and I think you have, this could be a sensational idea. Anyway, I am going to bed. I feel exhausted after the last couple of days.

'I think you're stable enough to sleep on your own tonight, don't you?' said Paul.

'Yes, I'm fine, better now than I've felt for years. I'll bring you up a cup of tea in the morning, but I will tell you now I'm not making a habit of it,' grinned Richard. 'Goodnight Paul and thanks.'

'Goodnight. Make yourself at home. *Mi casa es su casa*, remember.'

Richard sat down and relaxed. It was the first time he had been on his own since he arrived at Paul's. It was the first time he had had a chance to think. He wanted to stop what he was doing, of that he was sure. He also knew it was not going to be easy. When you had led the sort of life that he had been leading for the last ten years it would not be over just like that. Richard faced up to the fact that since he had arrived in London he had had sex with men every single day, except when he was on holiday. He was twenty-five and he knew that he could get pretty horny. It wasn't just cash that turned him on. What was he to do? He had decided to seek advice from a counselling service and perhaps safe sex would be a topic he could discuss. If it was just using a condom, that was not too bad. He knew that anal penetration was the most dangerous practice, and if either partner had AIDS, any fusion of body fluids could be lethal, even saliva, through kissing maybe. He would have to find out if he was going to stay with Paul.

Paul had been wonderful this weekend. Most people would have shown him the door after the first outburst. He had stood by him. He knew they would get on well when they first met. An actor; he grinned, but he liked the idea. He pictured himself as a star, arriving at award ceremonies at the Savoy or the Dorchester, with fans calling his name. He would have to change that; he was not going to be Dick Hard again. He thought about his real name, Richard Carter didn't sound too bad for a straight actor. Straight. What would happen if the studio wanted to link his name with an actress? He could see the headlines in the tabloids now. 'Gay actor at charity event with up-and-coming young actress.' I can't let on I'm gay. The public, even today, are very homophobic.

He laughed. Here he was, already a star and he hadn't even had an interview for drama school yet. Still, it was a nice dream. He made his way to bed. God, I feel randy, he thought.

Richard awoke at eight-thirty remembering his promise to Paul to take him some tea. He showered and slipped on a dressing gown. He went to the kitchen and started to prepare breakfast. He made up a tray and took it to Paul. He knocked and went in.

'Good morning, master,' said Richard. 'Here is your tea.' Richard handed Paul the tea and at the same time gave him one of his most devastating smiles.

'Stay away from me, or I'll ravish you here and now. I can't cope with you looking this good first thing in the morning. Particularly when I feel such an old boot,' laughed Paul. 'How did you sleep? I didn't hear you go to bed. Were you late?'

'Not very late. I had to think things through. It was the first time I had had to myself, and the last few days have been pretty traumatic for me,' said Richard.

Paul looked at him to see if he was being serious or flippant. 'What conclusions did you reach?'

87

'I have got to change my life style, but it isn't going to be easy. I'm twenty-five, I can't lead the life of a monk. I just know. I'm not like you, Paul, I can't control my feelings the way you have.'

'What you've never had, you never miss. An old but wise saying,' said Paul.

'I have also decided to go to a counselling service and talk to them. After all, I can't be the only horny bastard in London, can I?' said Richard.

'No, but I wouldn't be surprised if you're up there among the top ten,' laughed Paul. 'Something else has to be said. You don't have to stay with me, Richard. If you meet a guy nearer your own age and you want to go to live with him, I won't stop you. Not unless I think you're going back on the streets.'

'I don't know how to answer that. If I did find somebody else, I'm not sure that I would be prepared to give up seeing you. I want us to be friends and even go away on our own sometimes,' said Richard.

'You want me as a mistress you mean – you are a tart,' laughed Paul. 'Well, that's fine by me.' He looked at Richard who was sitting on the edge of the bed. 'I just want to see you happy and safe. I want to be a father to you as we said once before, and you can be the son I never had. It's something that gays miss, particularly when they get older: a family.'

'I do love you and I am sure we're going to be mates for years,' said Richard.

'I wouldn't mind if now and again you pose for me the way you used to pose for Chris,' said Paul shyly, turning slightly red.

Richard laughed, and as he turned to leave the room he dropped his dressing gown to the floor and posed for Paul in a very erotic manner.

They both laughed as they knew that they had sealed their relationship and both men understood the rules. As they stood at the moment anyway.

Chapter 6

Paul had driven Richard up to town and dropped him at the King's Road as he had asked. Richard walked the short distance to the garage to pick up his car. He then drove to his flat and let himself in. He looked around, everything was as he had left it. There was no reason why it shouldn't have been, of course, but so much had happened over the weekend it seemed as though he had been away longer. Richard wasted no time. He sorted out his two suitcases and a sports bag and started to pack his clothes. He found some black bin bags and filled them with bed linen, etc. He had made up his mind to leave the curtains and fittings, or as much as he could. They would be of no use to him living at Paul's. When the suitcases were packed he took them to the car park and loaded them into his car. He went back to the flat to look at what was left. Not much for ten years, he thought. He had a few books he wanted to keep, his music centre and CD collection. The television was rented. He would have to sort that out sometime. He started to empty the drawers. He came across the videos he had made. He had better hang on to those – someone might want a reference! He found some old photographs too. He started looking through them and the memories came flooding back. Richard found a picture of himself and Ken outside the local dance hall in Haywards Heath. I wonder who took that, he thought. Then remembered; they had been waiting for a couple of girls that they had chatted up the previous week. They hadn't turned up. He waited with Ken for over an hour. They finished up back at the village dance in Frogham. He suddenly thought of Patsy Fisher. It was the following Saturday that she had asked him to go outside with her after they had been dancing together. He couldn't help smiling as he remembered what had happened. He had never been so embarrassed in all of his life. Sweet innocence, he thought. Another picture was of him and Chris in the early days when they were still sharing a flat. They were certainly a couple of good-looking boys. Where did it go wrong? Why did I turn out to be a whore? Why did I turn out to be gay? He thumbed through the rest of the snaps and came across the pictures he had taken in the Seychelles. He would keep those to show to Paul. Richard put the pictures and his books and records into a bag ready to take to the car. He had one last look round and really didn't think there was anything he wanted to take to remind him of this flat. He had had too many one-night stands there for it to hold many happy memories. He made arrangements for a storage firm to collect the furniture and that was that. He left and shut the door. He went to his car and drove to the studio to see Chris. This he wasn't looking forward to. He still had no idea as to how Chris would react. He was soon to find out.

The traffic was not too bad and so Richard was parking his Vauxhall in Mayfair about half an hour later. He walked into the studio and asked the receptionist, Sarah, if Chris was in.

91

'Yes, I think so,' she said. 'The light is on in the back studio, so he must be filming, but I haven't seen him.'

'Thanks, I'll find him,' said Richard. He knew that if the light was on in that particular studio gay filming was going on and Chris was there. Richard wanted to talk to Chris alone but he wanted to let him know that he was here. He knocked on the door.

'Hi, it's me, Dick. Can I come in?'

'Yes, I want to see you. Where the hell have you been all weekend? I've been ringing you at your flat, and I've tried all of your usual haunts. Nobody had seen you since Friday.'

'I'm sorry, Chris, that's why I want to see you, but in private,' said Richard.

'Do you two mind, I can't stand here with a hard on for ever, you know.'

It was Chuck, one of Chris's top models.

'Sorry, Chuck, I know how you feel. Chris, I'll see you at Miranda's at one-thirty, OK?'

'What's up, kid, anything wrong? Anything I can do to help?' said Chris.

'No, it's all under control. I'll tell you about it at lunch. I warn you, you may not like what I'm going to say. So please listen to me before saying anything. See you at one-thirty. Sorry Chuck.' Richard left before Chris could start questioning him in front of Chuck. He said goodbye to Sarah and left the studio.

When he was outside in the fresh air he felt relieved, a weight off his shoulders. He had made a start. No going back now. He checked the time, it was twelve-thirty. What could he usefully do for an hour? Drive to RADA and see what he could find out about enrolment into the school.

Paul, after dropping Richard off, continued to Wardour Street in Soho. John Simmonds had a studio there where, as the Independent Production Company, he made programmes for television. Normally they were series but sometimes a movie. The two men had been friends for years. Paul had stayed weekends at John's home in Weybridge. He got on well with Ann, John's wife, and the three of them often had lunch or dinner together. John had worked for various television companies, which was where he and Paul had met. Now John had his own company and appeared to be doing very well. Apart from wanting to see John, Paul thought John would be able to say if Richard's joining RADA was a practical suggestion, or if, indeed, there was an easier way of getting started: making commercials, for example.

'Paul, good to see you again,' said John, shaking Paul's hand warmly.

'It's good to see you too, John. I've been gallivanting around the world again, you know me, can't keep still for very long,' said Paul.

'It certainly seems to agree with you. The rest of us are getting older, you seem to be getting younger.'

'That's because I mix with younger people now. I have to keep on my toes,' laughed Paul. 'That's partly why I'm here.'

'Yes, it all sounds very mysterious. You said over the phone that you wanted to talk business at me. What's it all about?' asked John.

'It's quite simple really. I met a man while I was on holiday – don't laugh when I tell you he's only twenty-five, he was one of the few English-speaking people I did meet. We got on very well right from the start and spent the best part of two weeks together. We got to know one another pretty well. He'd been having a rough time, personal troubles, and was trying to sort himself out. Well, to cut a long story short, he's a very good-looking guy and he wants to become an actor. I've got some photographs that I took while we were away. The camera likes him. I thought you might have some ideas on how he could break into show business, as they say.' Paul handed the pictures to John.

'What is the boy doing now, or what has he been doing?' said John still looking at the pictures.

'He's done some modelling and photographic work,' said Paul.

'Has he got a portfolio of the work that he's done, could I see anything of his?'

'I don't think so, but I'll ask him,' said Paul, who couldn't help a small smile crossing his face at the thought of Richard's portfolio.

'I can see what you mean, he is very handsome, but he's got something else too. He looks good in a snapshot but I wonder how he handles himself in front of a camera,' said John.

'I agree, I suggested that he try to get into RADA,' said Paul. 'He was over the moon about the idea.'

'Has this man got a name?' asked John.

'Richard Carter,' said Paul.

John looked at the pictures again. 'I've got a really terrible idea and I'm sure that my producer and casting director will go mad, but I want to try something. No point in being the boss if you can't do what you want to do, is there?' said John smiling. 'We're about to start a new series called *Streetcred*. It's about a young guy who has spent most of his life on the streets as his home life was a bad deal. He learns all the con tricks and lives by his wits. He is very much a loner and just keeps one jump ahead of the police. He sleeps rough sometimes, but he mostly seems to con someone into giving him a bed for the night, and a meal. Your boy has something else apart from good looks, something we've not been able to find so far. He has that look of confidence and assertiveness that a know-all kid would have. I'd like to see how he performs on camera and how he looks on screen. Just a minute, let me get a couple of people in here.'

John picked up the phone and asked if Alex and Kate could join him as soon as possible.

Paul sat there trying to take in all that was going on around him. A few minutes later a knock at the door and two people entered. John introduced them as Alex Smith, producer of *Streetcred*, and Kate Stevens, casting director. He introduced Paul as an old friend.

'I've got a crazy idea, and before you both go off half-cocked I want you to listen. Paul has a friend who wants to get into acting. He's had some experience as a model and has done some photographic work. I want you to look at these holiday photos and see what you think about young Mr Carter – his name is Richard Carter – as Tony.' John handed the pictures to Alex.

Alex looked at them. He looked up at John and then looked at the pictures again. 'I can see what you mean,' said Alex. 'He has got something that none of the others have shown.' He passed them to Kate.

'One thing he has got is sex appeal,' said Kate. 'He's a very handsome boy, but can he act, or more importantly, can he handle himself in front of the camera?'

Paul was longing to scream out, yes, of course he can. I've seen him, and without his clothes. But he did not say a word.

'I'd like to set up a screen test for him as soon as we can. Then we'll know if we should pursue this any further or not. What do you two think?' said John.

'I agree,' said Alex. 'Kate?'

'Yes, if he can act we might have found this generation's James Dean.'

'Great,' said John. 'Can I leave you to arrange the test, Alex. And, Paul, can you get in touch with the boy to get him here when we want him?'

'Simple,' said Paul. 'At the moment he's staying with me.'

Paul noticed the movement in the room which seemed to indicate, 'Oh, I see.' He was going to explain, but decided to hell with it. He would talk to Richard first so that they could work out a story if need be.

'Is there anything that Richard should do before he takes the test, like get an Equity card or register somewhere?' Paul asked.

'No, I'll look after all of that, it won't be a problem. Equity know that we've been looking to cast this part for weeks now,' said Kate. 'Just tell him to get a good night's sleep and not to wear any aftershave that is too sexy or the girls on the set will eat him alive,' she grinned.

'OK thanks, Kate, Alex. That's about it. You'll let me know what time the test is tomorrow, will you Alex?' said John.

'Yes, sure,' said Alex.

'Good. Paul and I are going to lunch. We might not be back, as we have a lot of catching up to do,' said John. 'Come on, my friend, you can take me to the best restaurant around here as a penalty for leaving it for so long.'

Paul laughed, and although he couldn't wait to tell Richard what had happened today, he was looking forward to lunch with an old friend he had not seen for some months.

96

Chris arrived at Miranda's just after one-thirty. Richard was already at the table waiting for him.

'Chris, hello,' said Richard. 'I'm sorry if I sounded mysterious earlier, but I'll explain after we've ordered.' Richard called the waiter and ordered for both of them: veal marsala and a bottle of Frascati.

'What's all this about?' asked Chris.' 'You seemed bothered. Are you in trouble, can I help?'

'No, it's nothing like that, but I don't think you're going to like what I'm going to say. So please, Chris, put your tolerant head on,' said Richard.

'Are you trying to tell me that I have a short fuse?' grinned Chris.

'Yes, that's why I thought I would buy you lunch. You aren't likely to have me beaten up on a full stomach,' smiled Richard.

'This is getting really intriguing,' said Chris, 'but I wish you would get on with it.'

Richard took a deep breath. 'I'm going to quit. I'm not making any more videos and I'm not working the streets. I'm finished,' he said.

Chris looked stunned. He stared at Richard, his mouth open and a fork full of food in mid-air.

'What in hell has brought this on?' said Chris, beginning to regain his composure. 'You haven't got religion all of a sudden, have you?'

'No. I decided to get out while I'm still young enough to find another career. I don't want to be a thirty-five-year-old rent-boy and even porno stars are past their sell-by date at that age,' said Richard, trying to assess how Chris was taking what for him must be a pretty devastating piece of news.

'What made you decide?' asked Chris.

'I met a guy when I was on holiday, he's really nice,

and it's not what you think. We got on very well and spent about two weeks together. He thinks that I'm a legitimate businessman in partnership with you, my old university friend, in a photographic studio in Bond Street. Or at least, he did. I thought when the holiday was over we would say goodbye and that would be that. Paul, that's his name, had other ideas. He wanted to meet me for lunch, have drinks, stay the weekend. I realised that I was in trouble. I couldn't meet Paul in London – in no time he would be suspicious as to what I was doing for a living. I decided to write to him so that he would have the letter at home when he got back from the rest of his holiday, saying that it wouldn't work if we were to meet and someone was bound to get hurt, which was the last thing I wanted. Paul tracked me down at the studio the other night. You remember we were filming and I had a call. I knew that I had to see him and to tell him the truth, so I did.'

'You told him everything?' asked Chris.

'Yes. I thought he would throw me out or even call the police. He didn't. He picked me up and beat the shit out of me. He told me what a fool I was and didn't I care how other people felt. It turns out that Paul's gay and has fallen in love with me. He is a latent gay, very much in the closet, even I didn't realise. We slept in the same bed that night. I put it that way because I don't want you to get the wrong idea. Paul comforted me and nursed me. You cannot begin to understand how I felt telling Paul, the one person who respected me for myself, that I was a whore and a porn star, that I'd been on the streets since I was sixteen. If Paul hadn't been there for me that night I might well have killed myself. There is one other hot piece of news that I should tell you. I'm HIV positive. It was confirmed just before I went to the Seychelles.'

98

'Richard, I'm so sorry. Where, how?' Chris never called him Richard, only Dick. He appeared genuinely shaken. 'What are you going to do?'

'Thanks. It was a blow to me too. It's always going to be someone else, isn't it. I'm now going to obliterate my past life, with the help of Paul. He said I should examine my assets and use them,' smiled Richard. 'I think he means that I'm good in front of the camera, and maybe I should try straight acting. So after a very traumatic weekend, I'm going to start a new life, what's left of it,' said Richard.

'Do you know where you became infected?' asked Chris.

'Yes, I'm pretty sure it was Peter le Fenn. I've always been for health checks, you know that, and I've been clear. It was only after he joined the team that I became infected. Let's face it Chris, we didn't know much about him – where he came from, what he'd been doing or with whom. He's always been very secretive about his past. I can't do anything about it now,' said Richard.

'No, but I can,' said Chris.

'Chris, I know this has been a shock to you, but are you prepared to help me?' asked Richard.

'Of course I am. We've been friends for a long time, kid, and somehow I feel responsible for you.'

'That's probably because you were the one to introduce me to this life,' grinned Richard.

'OK, smart arse. What do you want from me?' said Chris.

'I want the master tapes of all of the videos that I've featured in. I'll pay for them. I also want us to part friends,' said Richard.

'That's fair enough. I've got the masters at home. I don't

keep things like that around the office for any prying eyes to see,' said Chris.

'What are you going to do about the business?' asked Richard.

'I was wondering that myself. I think I can cover you on the photographic side. I've got a couple of boys I have got my eye on, I would like to have given them longer to work out in the gym. Never mind. The trouble is on the video side of the business. You were so good, not many guys have got what you have got, the looks, the body, the smile and the sexuality, and can still take directions from me,' said Chris.

'Can't you use one of the guys you are going to use for the photo sessions?'

'No. They're not old enough. They're both only seventeen and you know I won't use anybody under twenty-one,' said Chris.

'What about Chuck? I'm sure he'd love it,' said Richard.

'Yes, I was thinking about him too. I think you're right,' answered Chris.

'When can I collect the tapes, Chris?' asked Richard.

'I'll give you a call in a couple of days,' said Chris.

'You can't, remember. I'm not at the flat any more. I'll call you,' said Richard.

'Doesn't your friend Paul have a phone?'

'Sure, but I don't remember the number.' Richard somehow felt he didn't want to give Paul's phone number to anyone without asking Paul first.

'Well, some of us still have to work for a living, I must go, kid. It was a great lunch, and I'm pleased that you're happy about your future. Don't forget to ring now and again. I may even offer you a guest spot in my latest movie,' smiled Chris as he stood to shake hands with Richard.

'Thanks for everything, Chris. Over the years you've been a good friend to me. Other people wouldn't understand that. I'll phone to collect the tapes in a couple of days. Bye, Chris.' Chris went from the restaurant and Richard called the waiter for the bill.

That all seemed a bit too easy. Richard felt as if more was still to come, but he didn't know what. The waiter returned with the credit card slip and Richard signed and left.

Chris stormed into his office. 'Sarah, find Peter le Fenn and send him to me. Also get in touch with Jamie Price and Carl Bennet and have them fix an appointment to see me here tomorrow. And get Chuck to call in before he goes home.'

'Yes, Mr Clarke,' said Sarah as she was dialling the phone number for Peter le Fenn.

Peter le Fenn went into the office. 'Hi Chris, you wanted me?'

'I want you, you bastard. You have AIDS and you didn't tell me? Now a good friend of mine has been infected. From you. You're fired. You don't work for me again and I'll see to it that all other producers know that you're infected and see if you can get a job then. Get out!'

Peter le Fenn was so stunned he said nothing, he turned and walked out. He stopped at the door. 'I'm sorry, Chris, I really needed this job. I haven't worked since I was diagnosed HIV positive. I hoped that I wouldn't pass it on.'

'Get the fuck out of here!'

'Chuck, come in, sit down. I was pleased with the way the shoot went today. You're looking good. Do you still work out at the gym?' said Chris.

101

'I sure do. I like to look good and keep in shape,' said Chuck.

'I have a proposition to put to you; from time to time I make some movies, gay movies, I vet all my artists carefully to make sure that they're discreet and clean. If you're willing to have a test for AIDS and would like to use your talents in front of the camera, I'll give you a try.'

'Sure, Chris, that would be great. I take it there's more money,' said Chuck.

'Yes, you would get well paid, but you do realise that there would be more body contact with the other guys, not like standing for a picture in a magazine,' said Chris, thinking to himself, poor Chuck, he is a bit dumb really.

'Sure, Chris, I understand. Will I know the other guys?'

'If you don't at the beginning of the shoot, you sure as hell will at the end.'

The next day the red light was on in the back studio and Jamie and Carl were doing their first photo session. They looked good. Chris was pleased.

Chapter 7

Richard arrived home first. He waited impatiently for Paul. They had so much to discuss. The price of the tapes – Paul had said £1,500 per tape. Richard had been shocked that Paul was prepared to give him so much money. It was a considerable amount. He thought of what Chris had said and his visit to RADA.

He heard a car pull into the drive. He poured a couple of drinks and listened for Paul to close the garage before he went to open the door. Paul came in looking very flushed.

'What's the matter?' said Richard. 'You look very excited.'

'Nothing, just wait to hear what I have to tell you. It'll blow your mind,' said Paul. 'I need a drink.'

'I've poured you a scotch; it's over there,' said Richard. 'Come on, tell me what is going on.'

'OK,' Paul replied.

He sat down and started to tell Richard what had taken place at the studio. How he had shown John some photographs of Richard and of his reaction. He told how Alex and Kate had liked the look of him too, and about John's idea to screen test Richard for the part of Tony. When he had finished he said to Richard, 'Well, what do you think?'

Richard was dumb. He stuttered and stammered, he couldn't speak one word coherently. Eventually he said, 'I can't believe it. A screen test! What will I have to do? When is it? Paul, I'm so excited I can't think straight. Is my luck going to change? Suppose the screen test is all right, does that mean that I get the part of Tony? I can't act. I've never acted in my life, I thought that's why we agreed that I should apply to RADA. Why me, why haven't they cast a regular actor?' asked Richard only just about able to get out the words of all the questions that he wanted answered. Paul was laughing.

'If you jabber on like that nobody will be able to understand a word you say, and so goodbye screen test. Let's take this slowly. I take it that you are in favour of taking the screen test?' Paul held up his hand as Richard was about to speak. 'A rhetorical question. If they like you, yes, I think they're going to offer you the part of Tony. Why not an established actor? I got the impression that they're looking for a new face, an up-and-coming youngster. So far all the auditions have produced the same "new faces" as last year.

'John said to me that he could see in you the confidence and cockiness, the assertive manner that he was looking for. He said you looked like a street kid. Needless to say, I didn't add any comment,' said Paul.

'I'm overwhelmed,' said Richard. 'I still can't believe it. A whore one day and a star the next. What do we do now?' asked Richard.

'First, I think you should stop referring to yourself as a whore, one day you'll say it in front of someone other than me. And a star you ain't,' advised Paul.

'Yes, you're right, I must stop saying that. It's just that

104

I've never been so excited with all of my clothes on before,' grinned Richard.

'You're incorrigible,' smiled Paul.

'After what you've just said it makes my bit of news seem insignificant,' said Richard. 'I went to see Chris today.'

'Of course. I'd forgotten. How did you get on?' asked Paul.

'I went to the studio and made arrangements to see Chris for lunch. I told him I want out, and asked if I could buy the tapes. I didn't mention any money. You said £1,500, is that still OK? It's a lot of money,' said Richard.

'It's what we agreed, so let's stick to it,' answered Paul.

'Chris was surprised when I told him and worried about how he was going to replace me, but that's his problem. He asked me what had made me come to this decision and I told him about you. I hadn't intended to, but you are such a very important part of my life now that I couldn't help it,' said Richard.

'It doesn't matter. Did you tell him we were living together?' asked Paul.

'I told him I was staying at your house but that it wasn't a relationship. He asked if you knew about me. When I said yes, I had told you everything, he seemed surprised. I told him how you beat me up too,' said Richard grinning. 'He said I deserved it and that he should have done the same thing years ago. Chris is still and always will be a friend. We went through too much together when we were both teenagers.'

'How do you get the tapes?' asked Paul.

'I'm going to phone Chris in a couple of days. He doesn't keep stuff like that in the studio. Too many prying eyes, he said,' said Richard. 'He was really upset when I told him I was HIV positive. He asked me if I knew who

I might have caught it from. When I told him he went white with rage. I wouldn't like to be in that guy's shoes when Chris gets hold of him.'

'What else did you do today?' asked Paul.

'I went to RADA and asked about joining. I was told I'd have to be interviewed, given my experience on the stage, and would have to do a reading, but first I must fill in an application form and if I got that accepted the interview would follow. "But you must realise, young man, we have 200 applicants a month, you'll have to be exceptional to get a place here." "I am," I told her, collected a form and left,' said Richard.

'Let's go out to eat tonight. I'm too hyped up to cook,' said Paul.

'Good idea, but only if it's my treat,' said Richard.

'I see. Acting like a Hollywood star already, are we? An advance on what you'll be earning when you are starring opposite Nicole Kidman,' said Paul.

'I'd rather be starring opposite Tom Cruise,' smiled Richard.

'Down boy. We all know what you want,' said Paul. 'Come here.'

Paul rang John as soon as was decent after breakfast to say that he had spoken to Richard, who was over the moon at being asked to do a screen test. John said it had been arranged for that afternoon with Alex, and could he and Richard be at the studio at two p.m.

Paul relayed this information to Richard, who by now was a total wreck. Paul laughed. He had never seen Richard like this, he was always so in control, so confident. He had suddenly become a teenager, brash and aggressive, but with no self-confidence. Paul knew that

Richard had grown from puberty to manhood almost overnight when he got off the train at Victoria.

'Paul, what will I have to do? What should I wear? Do you think I should wear a suit and tie or something casual? Slacks and a jumper. Maybe I should wear jeans and a tee-shirt, after all, it is that sort of part, isn't it? Oh Christ, I'm so nervous, I don't know what's the matter with me,' said Richard.

'You're growing up. You're going through what most eighteen and nineteen-year-olds go through when something important is about to happen to them. For you, it's happening at twenty-five. Just think about the agonies that they are going through learning about sex and love and how proficient you were at that by the time you were nineteen,' said Paul, acting like a father. 'I think you should wear something casual. Slacks, a plain blue shirt – white screws up in the lights for television – and a jumper if you like, but don't try to look like your all-American boy. It might be better if you wore your bomber jacket. Don't worry. Just be yourself, relax. You know that you have plenty of confidence and charm. Use it, use that killer smile of yours. If you don't get this part, it may lead to something else. You've got nothing to lose. Just remember, you don't have to take your clothes off for this test, so if the cameraman is cute, don't get carried away,' said Paul laughing.

'Very funny,' smiled Richard. 'There is one thing I think we should talk about. Who am I? What is our relationship exactly and what have I been doing? I know that you said that I had done some modelling, but will that do?'

'I don't see why not, at least for the time being. All they're interested in is how you look in front of the camera. You have an easy personality, let things take their course,' said Paul.

107

'What about us, what do I say? How well does John know you?'

'If you mean does he know that I'm gay, no. At least, we don't talk about it. I have known John and his wife for over twenty years. If you say something that can be misinterpreted, don't worry. It'll be something for John and me to sort out. I told him the truth as far as I could. That we met on holiday and spent a couple of weeks together, and that now, because of personal reasons, you wanted to give up modelling and try to become an actor. How you handle people is up to you. If you want to be straight, fine. If you want people to know that you're gay, that's fine too. However, I would be grateful if you corrected ideas anyone might have about us being lovers,' said Paul.

'That goes without saying,' said Richard. 'I'm going to have a bath. No peeking,' he ducked a blow from Paul that, if it had connected, would have given him a hefty whack round the ear. He laughed. 'Missed.'

Paul grinned. I'm behaving like a stupid schoolboy with this young man. I must be more careful when John's around. Oh, to hell with it. At my age I'll do what I damn well like. Not that I'm doing anything, anyway. God, this is so confusing. Love. Who needs it?

Paul went to change. He wanted to leave by twelve-thirty to allow plenty of time for traffic and parking.

Richard had been very quiet in the car and so Paul had not said much either. Paul thought Richard was nervous, and it was better for him to be nervous now than at the studio. Richard was actually thinking up a background for himself. Enough to tide him over today, at least. Did he have a girlfriend or was he married? Where did he live? What work had he done before? All ordinary questions that he might be asked by anybody. He needed a story.

'You've been very quiet. Don't worry, you'll be fine,' said Paul.

'No, it's not that. I've been making a cover story for myself. As a matter of fact, I'm not a bit nervous now. I'm going in there and blowing the socks off 'em,' he said in his typically self-confident manner.

'That's my boy. Well here we are. The best of luck. Just smile at them the way you smile at me and you will have them eating out of your hand,' said Paul. 'Come on, or we'll be late.'

They entered the studio and asked the receptionist for Mr Simmonds.

'Are you Mr Green and Mr Carter?' she asked, not taking her eyes from Richard.

'Yes, we are,' said Paul.

'Mr Simmonds said he'll be a couple of minutes. Would you like to take a seat,' she said.

'Thanks.'

'Would you like some coffee? It's from a machine I'm afraid,' apologised the receptionist.

'Not for me thanks,' said Paul.

'I would like some please, black, no sugar,' smiled Richard.

Paul watched and could not believe the way the girl went completely to pieces when Richard looked at her and smiled. Richard hadn't noticed a thing. I suppose being gay he isn't aware of how women react to him or doesn't care. I bet he would pick up on any boy who walked through reception and looked at him twice.

Kate and Alex got out of the lift and came towards Paul.

'Hi, Paul, John's over at the set. If you would like to

come with me and Kate, we'll take you over. This, I take it, is Richard Carter,' said Alex, holding out his hand towards Richard. 'I'm Alex Smith and this is Kate Stevens.'

'Yummy,' said Kate.

'Don't take any notice of her, she hasn't had her daily dose of teenagers yet,' laughed Alex.

Richard shook hands with both of them, grinned, and said, 'Sorry Kate, I'm well past my teens, but if I can help I'll try my best.'

'You and I are going to get on, I can see that,' said Kate 'Come on, you beautiful creature. Make-up. Let's see if we can't do something about those looks and make you more like a mortal than a god.'

Richard turned on the full charm this time, gave her the full Carter smile and offered her his arm as they walked down the corridor. Paul could hear squeals of laughter coming from Kate and he knew that Richard wasn't nervous now. He looked at Alex. 'What's next?'

'You and I will go to the control room and I'll show you what's going to happen. We'll be able to watch all that's going on but neither Richard nor anybody else will be able to see or hear us,' said Alex.

'I must say, Paul, that boy has got charm. I've never seen Kate react like that before, and even I can appreciate his good looks. A bit pretty boy, but he's still quite macho. I hope he does a good test. He's perfect for the part of Tony. In some ways he looks like a street kid,' said Alex.

'Yes, I don't think he is as innocent as he sometimes makes out,' said Paul. 'After all, he is twenty-five.'

'Has Richard got any acting experience?' asked Alex, 'because if things go well today, we could probably get him into a good school. It's one that we have used before in similar circumstances.'

110

'To the best of my knowledge, he's never acted before. He was a model. Fashion, that sort of thing, and he's done some photographic work. Stills. For posters and brochures rather than commercials,' answered Paul.

'What do you think, would he like to go to drama school?' asked Alex.

'I would think he'd consider giving up sex for it,' laughed Paul.

'Pretty serious then,' grinned Alex. 'Here we are: Control Room B. Richard will be testing down there. As I said, he can't see us, although somehow I don't think it would worry him if he thought we could,' said Alex.

'What will he have to do?' asked Paul, who was sure that he was far more nervous than Richard might be.

'First, I want to see what he looks like on screen. The big close-up, which can be a killer. We'll be moving the camera around so that we can have different angles of Richard. Some flattering, some not so flattering. I want to see how he moves on camera too. Some people are so clumsy when they're told to do something rather than doing something of their own volition. If all of that goes well I'll want him to read for me. I might even get Mandy Rider, she is the female lead in *Streetcred*, to play a short scene with Richard. She's standing by.'

Paul wished he had never asked, he would be exhausted by the time this was all over.

Kate walked into Make-up with Richard still on her arm.

'This,' she announced to everybody, 'is my new boyfriend, his name is Richard Carter. Isn't he beautiful?'

'Don't be such a cow, darling, you're embarrassing the boy,' said Pat, who was the senior make-up artist.

'Richard, baby, I'm not embarrassing you, am I?' asked Kate.

111

'I have been in worse situations. Not many though, and not with such pleasant company,' smiled Richard.

'You see what I mean. He's wonderful. Darling, I hope that you can act. But I don't care if you can't, I'm going to cast you anyway,' said Kate.

'Yes, alone, with you on a desert island,' said a voice from one of the make-up cubicles.

'I'm not sure he's your type, Michael. Pat, I'll leave my new find with you and if there is a mark on him when I get back I'll tear you limb from limb. I know it'll be difficult but try to make him look less like Adonis,' said Kate. 'He's due on set in fifteen minutes. Bye, Richard, I shall be watching your every move, and I bet you've got some good ones.'

'I bet I've got some you have never seen,' said Richard and gave Kate a lascivious wink.

Kate was blushing when she left to go to the Control Room.

As she entered Control Room B, Kate said, 'That boy may look like an angel, but I think he has a very dirty mind.'

Paul and Alex looked at each other, but decided not to ask any questions.

Kate Stevens was thirty-five years old and had been working in television and films all of her working life. She had never married; she had never found it necessary for sex and she couldn't for the life of her think of any other reason to marry. She had worked with John for ten years. They worked well together and so she had followed him when he went independent. She hadn't regretted it for one minute. Kate was looking forward to *Streetcred* going into production; it was her first big series. Richard Carter was Tony; in her mind there was no doubt. She

112

also had no doubt that Mr Carter would perform beauti-
fully in front of the camera, and that Alex would be
delighted, and that Richard would be hired.

The test was about to start. Paul was so tense that he
was beginning to sweat. He stared at the stage waiting
for Richard and wishing it was all over. Richard came on
stage and the director placed him by a bar which made
up part of the set. He spoke to Richard but they couldn't
hear what was being said in the Control Room. Richard
took his jacket off and carried it over his shoulder, he had
his other hand in his pocket. He rested himself against a
bar stool with one foot on the rung of the stool. The
camera moved in close and backed off. Again the camera
travelled towards Richard but this time from the side. All
the time Alex was watching the screen, making notes,
murmuring to his PA now and again.

The director yelled 'cut', and everybody relaxed.

'Good, that was fine, Richard,' he said. 'Now I want to
see how you respond to my directions. I want you to take
up the same position at the bar. Then, on my word I want
you to make as though you were leaving. Put your coat
on and walk towards the door. While you're doing that I
may ask you to do something else. You follow what I tell
you, got that?' he asked.

'Sure,' said Richard.

'Good, take up your first position.'

The camera was already rolling. The director wanted to
see how Richard behaved when he thought the cameras
were not on him, as well as when they were. Alex and
Kate could not take their eyes from him now. This was
the real test.

Richard walked over to the bar in a relaxed manner, he
took off his jacket and casually tossed it over his shoulder
and put his hand in his pocket, sat down on the bar stool

113

and waited for directions as to what he was to do next. He smiled towards the Control Room. Someone had told him that they would be watching from there.

The director said, 'OK Richard, finish your drink and leave by the main door.'

Richard picked up a glass that had appeared on the bar and swallowed the air which was the only thing there was in it. He put the glass down and said goodnight and gave a little wave to an imaginary barman. He walked across the stage to the door.

'Cut.'

Richard turned to the director. 'Was that all right?'

'That was good. This time do it again but as you get half-way to the door feel in your pocket as if you were looking for something and finding it's not there go back to the bar to see if you can find it. Understand?'

'Yes. Do you want me to start from the entrance or from the position at the bar?' asked Richard.

'Do the entire thing again, it's looking good.'

After Richard had done that Alex said, 'Let's take a break for ten minutes. Then, Richard, I would like you to read to me. I'll come down and find some suitable dialogue.'

Paul looked at Alex and the expression in his eyes must have shouted out what he wanted to know.

'He's good, Paul. Very good. You were right, the camera likes him. I'm going to give him a chance to read now and I'm certainly going to get him to do a scene with Mandy. Kate, I think we've found Tony.' Kate just smiled at Paul who was grinning like a proud father at his son's graduation.

Richard was obviously not used to reading aloud, and this did not go as smoothly as the rest of the test. He read too slowly and stammered. He did have a nice sounding voice, though, which was the main thing. The scene with Mandy was much more successful. This time Richard had time to learn the words. He didn't falter and he was not reading too slowly. He followed Mandy in her moves and reacted to the way she played the part. She was flirting with him, trying to get him to pick her up. Make Mandy a guy, and it wasn't a million miles from what Richard had been doing for years.

It was over. Richard felt happy that he had done his best and he was quietly confident that his best was going to be good enough. He went back to the make-up department to remove the stuff that Pat had plastered on him. He was asked to join Paul, Alex and Kate in John's office after he had cleaned himself up.

Richard thought the make-up department would be bustling with people as it had been earlier. It wasn't. In fact, he thought he was the only person there. He sat down in front of a mirror and tried to wipe his face clean.

'Hi. I know you from somewhere,' said Michael.

Richard jumped. 'Christ, I didn't think there was anybody here. I don't think we've met. You're Michael, aren't you, the one who put Kate down?'

'Yes, she's OK, but she can be a bit of a bitch where gays are concerned, and I'm gay, and now I remember where I know you from.'

Richard's heart beat a bit faster, was his past catching up with him already?

'Where is that? The place that you remember me?' asked Richard.

'Before I answer I would like to ask you a few questions first,' said Michael.

'If that's part of the deal, and I'll tell you if I'm not prepared to answer them,' said Richard.

115

'Are you trying to get into the theatre seriously, or is it all a bit of a joke?'

'I am trying to start a new life and this acting job is what I really want to do,' said Richard.

'Are you gay?'

'Yes, why do you ask?'

'Are you going to pretend that you're straight as far as everyone around here is concerned?'

'I don't know. I've never been a badge-wearing gay who goes on all the gay rights marches or anything like that. I prefer to live and let live. I won't deny it but I won't advertise it either,' said Richard. 'I still don't understand the reason for these questions, and you still haven't said where you met me.'

'I was a customer of yours,' said Michael. 'I paid you twenty pounds.'

Richard went white. 'I see, I hope you thought it was worth it,' he said. 'But where does that leave us now? Are you going to tell Mr Simmonds?'

'No, you gave the right answers. If you'd denied that you were gay or had said that you were going to pretend to be straight, I might have done,' said Michael. 'I'm not a badge-wearing gay either, but I can't stand the hypocrisy that abounds in this business. I take it you've given up being a rent-boy.'

'Yes.' Richard had a sick feeling in his stomach.

'In that case I think you could need a friend around here, someone you can relax with and talk to. I would like to be that friend, and I promise you that I'll never say a word about how we met,' said Michael. 'By the way, yes it was worth it, every penny. You were very good to me. At the time I was really down. I'd just realised what I was and I didn't know who I could talk to or how I was going to cope with it. I knew that I wouldn't get any support from my parents or family. You let me talk and you gave me some good advice. I'll always be grateful. After that first time I looked for you lots of times – I think I was in love with you – I never did find you until now. I hope we can be friends, Richard.'

'Sure we can, Michael. Perhaps we can go for a drink sometimes too,' said Richard, more relieved than he was prepared to admit.

Richard cleaned himself up and Michael directed him to John's office. He knocked and went in. Kate was the first to rush up to him and gave him a big kiss.

'Darling, you were wonderful, you look even more beautiful on screen,' she said.

'Thank you, kind lady,' grinned Richard. He looked over towards Paul and gave him a half smile. Paul looked at Richard and their eyes met and said 'later'. Later we can talk and celebrate.

Alex stood up and said, 'I would like to make an announcement. I think we have found Tony for *Streetcred*. I give you Mr Richard Carter. I hope it all goes as well as it did today.' Cheers and applause went around the room, everyone in turn congratulating Richard and wishing him luck.

'Richard,' said Alex, 'I've spoken to Paul and he said you would like to go to acting school. I can get you into a good one and I can include it in your contract, if you agree, that the company will pay any expenses incurred. Are you appointing Paul as your manager? If so, if you and Paul could come into the office tomorrow we can sort out all the paperwork and arrange for your salary to be paid.'

'Yes, I'd certainly like to go to acting school and I'd like Paul to be my manager. I'll have to ask him. All being well we'll be in the office in the morning. Thank you,

Alex, I am grateful. One day you may know how much,'
said Richard.

'Good. Come on, let's have a drink.'

On the way home Richard told Paul about Michael and
Paul asked if Richard remembered him. Richard looked
sadly at Paul and said, 'He was one of many. How am I
expected to remember all of the guys that I've slept with?
It made me think when he said he was one of my customers. I realised just how vulnerable I am. They remember me, but I don't remember them. Any time someone
could say something.'

'I think that is one of the things you're going to have
to get used to,' said Paul.

'I know. I don't think there's a problem with Michael.
I think he's still lonely and when I said that we could go
for a drink occasionally, he was really excited.'

'Today has certainly been a day to remember. I can't
wait to get to bed, I'm knackered,' said Paul.

'Yes, same here,' said Richard, thinking to himself, it's
not just bed I want, it's someone in it. I don't know how
much longer I can carry on like this.

Paul couldn't sleep. He kept thinking of what John had
said to him in a quiet moment at the party. John had
tactfully found out that Richard was living with Paul,
although Paul was able to convince John that they were
not lovers. He had made Paul admit that he was gay and
Paul had told John that Richard was gay and that he had
been active. None of these things he had intended to say.
John had been sympathetic and had apologised for prying
into Paul's personal life. John had claimed that he wanted
to know about Richard, as he had seen problems arise
before with a gay pretending to be straight. He said he

could arrange escorts for Richard at social events if or when it became necessary. He could also make sure that the scripts did not make it too embarrassing for Richard by involving him in heavy love scenes. Paul had felt extremely uneasy while this cross-examination was taking place, and despite John's assurances that everything would be the same between Paul and John and his wife, Ann, Paul knew that they would never be the same. From now on he would be on his guard.

Chapter 8

Paul and Richard arrived at John's office at about eleven. John was expecting them and had all the paperwork ready. Richard signed a contract for the series with an option to make another two over two years. A clause was written in to allow Richard to attend acting classes at the expense of the studio, for a maximum period of a year. Alex had arranged for Richard to start at the school straight away, and Kate had made Richard a fully paid-up card-carrying member of Equity.

The formalities over, John phoned Alex and asked him to show Richard around and to introduce him to everybody. Richard stood up and shook hands with John and thanked him for giving him such a wonderful opportunity; he nodded towards Paul and said he would see him later. Alex and Richard left.

Paul also thanked John and made an excuse about how busy he knew John must be and left too.

Alex and Richard walked to the set of *Streetcred*. As rehearsals had not started yet, only the stagehands and carpenters were working. Alex told all who could hear who Richard was and that he was going to play the part of Tony. They all wished him luck and looked forward to working with him over the next few months.

'How do you feel, now that it's for real?' asked Alex.

'I still can't really believe it. I think I'll be better when we actually start rehearsing,' said Richard.

'Good, I'm glad you feel like that. If you come with me I'll get you a script. Read it, but don't try to learn all the lines immediately. Get a feeling of the part, decide on the character of Tony. What's he like? Is he a thug, or is he a con man? What? Try to understand him and his relationship with the other parts. Then learn your lines,' said Alex grinning. 'Don't worry, you'll get a lot of help from the director.

'We're starting tomorrow at nine-thirty. Luckily you're not required for some of the earlier scenes so it'll give you a chance to watch what goes on and to learn your lines. You met Mandy Rider yesterday at the test. How did you get on?' asked Alex.

'As far as I could tell, OK. I think we would need to talk to each other off the set first before I could give an in-depth appraisal,' said Richard with a smile.

'Right. Well, here is the script and I'll show you to the canteen and leave you to yourself. We don't need you until nine-thirty tomorrow, as I said, so you can stay here or go home. Some people can't study at home, others can. This is our humble canteen, I'll see you later. I really am pleased that it worked out so well, Richard. I think we could become friends. If either of us ever get the time to make friends,' said Alex.

'Thanks, I'd like that Alex. I think we could hit it off together too,' said Richard. 'See you later.' Richard looked at the script and felt his stomach start churning. It was excitement not fear, he hoped. He bought a cup of tea and a sandwich and looked for somewhere to sit.

121

'Hi, does this mean that you're working here permanently now?' It was Michael.

'Hello,' said Richard. 'I think it does. Do you mind if I join you?'

'No, great. Sit down,' said Michael.

'What are you working on?' asked Michael.

'*Streetcred*. I'm playing the part of Tony, a cocky know-all kid. It sounds just like me,' grinned Richard.

'Have you done any acting before?'

'Not even a school play,' said Richard.

'How did you get a chance to audition?' asked Michael curiously.

'I have a friend, a guy I met on holiday, and he and John Simmonds are old mates. Paul got me the chance. He showed some photographs of me that he had taken in the Seychelles to John and Alex Smith, and Kate Stevens who agreed that I was what they were looking for as Tony,' Richard explained.

Michael looked at him. 'I can see what they mean. Damn, you are a good-looking guy, Richard. Here's hoping that you can act,' he laughed.

'They're not taking any chances on that score, I'm being sent to acting school. I know, I'm a lucky bastard,' said Richard.

'You do seem to have fallen on your feet,' said Michael.

'Don't get me wrong, but are you jealous?' asked Richard.

'Hell, no. I was stating a fact. The last thing I ever wanted was to appear in front of a camera. I like working in make-up. It's not just powder and paint – think about things like the *Elephant Man*. It's also pretty hard if someone has to be aged, to get them to look the same every day. They don't keep their make-up on, you know,' said Michael.

122

'Good. I'd like us to be friends, Michael. I'm sure you could help me a lot. Identifying the scene helps, like you did yesterday with Kate. Do you fancy a drink before you go home tonight?' suggested Richard. 'I could use one, today has been quite a day for me.'

'That would be great, I shall be finished here at about six o'clock. I'll meet you at the reception desk. The pub around the corner is quite good. It's not a gay pub though, if that's what you want.'

'That's not what I want. I just want to go for a drink with a mate after work,' said Richard.

Michael smiled and said he would see Richard later, as he left the canteen.

Richard thought of Michael and grinned. He seems a nice bloke, a bit lonely, one who hasn't really accepted that he is gay, and obviously thinks that I'm something special. Perhaps we could have a bit of fun if it doesn't go too far. He's not a bad looking guy, a bit feminine, but not too bad. We'll see, thought Richard.

He opened the script and started to read. It was good. The story was interesting and moved along quickly. He was beginning to get a feeling for Tony. He was very much as he had been himself, except that Tony was not a rent-boy. Richard looked at the part Mandy Rider played and her relationship with Tony. It was obvious that Tony and Susie, Susie being Mandy's part, were going to become an item. Richard had been given only the first episode of the series and so he did not know how far any love scenes went. He wasn't worried about doing a love scene with a girl. What he was worried about was that he might do it too well, and even worse, he might make it very apparent that he had acted without clothes before.

He decided that he would not announce that he was gay, he would play it by ear. He wouldn't make a secret of having a drink with Michael, but he would still take any of the girls out if the opportunity arose. He would have to talk to Paul. Paul was an expert at being a 'straight' gay. Sometimes women just wanted an escort.

It was coming up to six p.m. when he was due to meet Michael. Richard left the canteen and went to the main reception. Michael was waiting for him. Richard slapped him on the back and they started for the door.

'Careful, Richard. You don't know where he's been. If you did you might not like it,' said Kate.

'Kate, I know exactly where he's been, and I think he has very good taste. Goodnight,' said Richard. Michael grinned.

Michael and Richard continued to the pub. They had a couple of drinks and chatted. Michael thanked Richard for sticking up for him against Kate. Richard, for his part, expressed some doubt as to his feelings towards Kate, whom he had at first liked. They left the pub with the casual 'cheers, see you tomorrow'.

'Not to worry. I thought I liked Kate, but I'm beginning to have my doubts,' said Richard. 'See you tomorrow. Cheers.'

Michael arrived at his Bayswater flat at about eight-thirty p.m. It was the best night he had had for a long, long time. He thought of Richard and immediately his heart beat faster and he felt hot, then he felt horny. He knew, inevitably, where this was going to lead. He had never forgotten Richard. He had been the man he had sex with for the first time. It wasn't only the sex, he liked Richard and who had been sympathetic towards him, as if he understood exactly what he was going through. He was twenty-two then. Michael had not had a lover, but he had asked a few friends round from time to time. He would have liked a long-term relationship. Perhaps Richard was the one. Michael was slowly undressing, he took his shoes and socks off, his tie, his shirt, his trousers. He stood in his boxer shorts looking at himself in the mirror. He thought of Richard as he took off his shorts. His hands caressed his body and he was lost in a world of fantasy.

He lay on the bed breathing heavily and shaking. He had not enjoyed himself so much for ages. Richard Carter certainly turned him on. He got up and went for a shower.

Richard told Paul all about his first day as an actor when he arrived home. He showed him the script and panicked about learning all his lines. He told Paul how Alex had shown him around and that he had said he thought he and Richard could be friends. He told Paul about Michael and what a bitch Kate had been. He said he thought Michael was in love with him. 'Aren't we all,' responded Paul.

He said that he had been for a drink with Michael and he could see that Michael was ecstatic. Richard then asked Paul how he managed to be straight with women and take them to dinner and not get involved. Paul said it was not something that he thought about. Paul had not had lovers so it seemed a fitting end to an evening that he escorted the lady home and then went home himself.

Richard said, 'That may be possible for you Paul, but I don't think I am going to be able to keep celibate for much longer.'

They both went to bed. It had been a long day for each of them and it would be an early start for Richard.

Richard went to his room and while undressing thought of Michael. The more he thought about him the harder he got until the usual happened. Perhaps this is how I am going to enjoy sex from now on, he pondered.

He went to sleep happy and contented.

The next day rehearsals started for *Streetcred*. Richard had never felt so nervous in all his life. He sat and watched as the first few scenes were played. The lights, the directions, the cameras, it was all so exciting and at the same time frightening. He had learnt his lines, at least for the early scenes, and he had understood the stage directions written in the margin of the script. Suddenly it was his turn. Some disembodied voice was asking him to take up his position for scene four. He froze. He couldn't move. He heard people shouting again – his name. Alex came over to him.

'What's the matter, didn't you hear? They're calling for you.'

'I can't. I can't remember a word, I can't move, I'm frozen. I think I'm going to be sick. Alex, I'm sorry, but I can't do this,' said Richard.

'Don't be such a prat. Of course you can. Come on, get up. I'll take you to the spot, once you're on the set you'll be fine,' said Alex. 'I'll buy you a drink tonight if you do a good job.'

Alex led Richard to his position on the set, whispered his first few lines, and shouted 'action'.

Richard opened his mouth and the right words came out. The rehearsal went pretty well. Richard soon got over his attack of nerves, and when he did he proved to have the makings of a good actor. Alex was pleased with the first day and said so to all the cast. He was particularly pleased with the way Richard and Mandy were getting on. They seemed to like each other, and that always helped. He was surprised that Richard hadn't made a

126

play for Mandy. He appeared to be the type who liked to make a conquest as soon as possible, to establish his credentials perhaps. Alex remembered how he had walked off arm-in-arm with Kate and he had only known her for an hour or so. Perhaps he was worried about the part and was going to play it cool as far as girls were concerned for the time being. Alex suddenly remembered he had said that he would take Richard for a drink if rehearsals went well. He had better find him to make the arrangements.

'There you are,' said Alex as he entered the make-up department. 'I promised to buy you a drink if I was satisfied with the way the rehearsals went. Apart from some prat who couldn't stand up or remember a single line, and I hope he's left us forever, I didn't think it was too bad. What do you think, Richard?'

'I'm so sorry, I feel such an idiot. I don't know what happened to me, I've never dried up like that before. I'm sure you're right, Alex. That guy has gone for ever, and, thank you, I would like to go for a drink,' said Richard.

'OK,' said Alex. 'I'll see you in reception at six o'clock.' Alex left and Richard continued to take his make-up off.

'Hello,' said Michael. 'I just wanted to say that I had a really good time last night. I don't go out much, so it made a nice change.'

'So did I,' said Richard, 'I'm going for a drink with Alex tonight, so we can't do it again, but another time if that's all right with you.'

'Yes, any time,' said Michael. 'Perhaps you would like to come back to my flat and I'll cook us some dinner.'

'Sounds great. How about Friday? I'll bring a bottle of wine and you can fill me in on all the gossip and politics,' said Richard. 'Then the next time you must come to my place and meet Paul.'

127

'Who's Paul?' Michael's face dropped at the mention of another man.

'Paul's my friend, not my lover. I live at his house for the moment. Paul's about fifty-five and he's been very good to me. More than you can imagine. One day I might tell you all about it. But for the moment let's say your place next Friday, and when I've checked with Paul, my place,' said Richard. 'I thought I'd spoken about Paul before. He's the guy who's a friend of John Simmonds and helped to get me the audition.'

'That's right, I remember now,' said Michael, instantly looking happier. 'I'm looking forward to our dinner date. Things are really beginning to pick up. I'd better go home now and give the flat a good clean.' he laughed.

'I expect I'll see you tomorrow, but if I don't, see you on Friday. Cheers,' said Richard.

'Bye', said Michael, gazing after Richard as if he could hardly believe his luck. The guy he had loved for years actually coming to dinner. Could he form a long-term relationship with Richard, he wondered.

Richard found somewhere quiet to learn his lines for the next day and also to try to understand the stage directions he might be given.

'Hi!' It was Mandy Rider. This is a popular place to get away from it all, he thought.

'Hi, yourself,' said Richard smiling. 'I thought that I'd find a place where I could be quiet and try to learn my lines. Then hopefully I won't make such a fool of myself again.'

'That's really why I came looking for you,' said Mandy. 'Don't bother about this morning, after that first bit of stage fright, you were great. I'm not just saying that to boost your confidence, you've got plenty of that.'

'Ouch. Is that a back-handed compliment?'

'No,' said Mandy, 'it's the truth. You were very good. I think we'll make a good team. I can relate to you. One of these days we might go for a drink.'

'Everybody is asking me to go for a drink. I'll be an alcoholic before long at this rate!' said Richard.

'Don't jest. It does happen a lot in this business,' said Mandy.

'I would love to have a drink with you sometime, as long as the boyfriend doesn't mind. Or is it the husband?' asked Richard.

'It isn't either, I'm a free agent and open to offers,' said Mandy.

'I'll remember that,' said Richard, now on his guard. He hadn't heard a more blatant come-on since he had last used it himself.

'You know where I am if you want me,' said Mandy.

'Yes,' said Richard. 'Behind the bike sheds?' looking at Mandy with an angelic expression.

'Bastard,' she said and walked out.

Oh dear, thought Richard, I must watch my step there. This isn't going to be easy. Perhaps I should let it be known that I'm gay and like it that way. Maybe he would find out more about the sexual politics tonight in the pub from Alex.

Richard studied for the next two hours without any interruptions and so he felt that he knew his lines well enough and understood the stage directions. He looked at his watch to discover that it was nearly six o'clock – time to meet Alex. He packed up his belongings and made his way to reception.

'How are you finding it being an actor?' grinned Alex.

'I don't know about being an actor, but what I've done so far I love,' said Richard.

'Have you made any friends?' asked Alex.

'Yes, a lot really. I don't know if you know him, but Michael from the make-up department and I were in this very pub last night. I'm seeing him for dinner on Friday, and he's coming to me next week,' said Richard.

'You want to be careful. Michael is gay,' said Alex.

'Yes I know, but I am big enough to look after myself if the need arises,' said Richard. 'Does it bother you that Michael's gay?'

'Not at all,' said Alex. 'I just thought you should know. Let's face it, you're a good-looking guy, I could fancy you myself.'

If that's not a come on, I'm straight, thought Richard. How did he react though that was the question. 'Are you trying to pick me up?' he whispered.

'What do you mean?' said Alex. 'I was making a statement that's all.' Alex turned away from Richard as he was by now a bright crimson.

'Don't worry, Alex, I'm gay, but I didn't know how to play it here. I would like us to know each other a lot better. Can't we be friends?' asked Richard.

Alex was still embarrassed. 'I've never done this before. I don't suppose that you believe me, but I don't know what I mean. I would like to be friends though.'

'Funnily enough, Alex, I do believe it is the first time that you've done that. I think we should forget about it for the time being. However, now that one thing is out in the open, I would like to pick your brains on who is sleeping with whom. I'm gay, as I've said, but I'm not going round shouting it from the roof tops, but on the other hand I'm not going to pretend to be straight. My sexual preference has nothing to do with other people, except my partner. I know Michael is gay and I know Kate is anti-gay. I'm not sure about you. Mandy made a

130

pass at me today which couldn't have been more obvious. What's the score?' asked Richard.

Alex had regained his composure. He was not embarrassed, probably more relived that such a stupid remark had been passed off so easily.

'Mandy is the easiest lay in the studio; everybody knows it too. Basically she's a slag. Michael is a nice boy. Boy, he's about twenty-seven, I suppose. He keeps himself to himself but he does do a lot of shouting about gay rights, which is a pain. You're right about Kate, she is very homophobic, I don't know why. I'm surprised that you knew,' said Alex.

'I heard her a couple of times having a dig at Michael,' said Richard. 'That leaves you, Alex.'

'I don't know about me. I have had a few affairs with women, after all, I am thirty. Just,' he added grinning. 'They didn't work. We got on all right as friends but in bed it was av'ful. I didn't enjoy it and I didn't satisfy my partners. And I don't know why I'm telling you this,' said Alex.

'You don't have to tell me a thing. What you do say is between you and me. I'm not a gossip, I just love to hear it,' smiled Richard. 'Sometimes talking can help to understand a problem. If it's a person that you don't know that well, it can be easier. Relax, Alex.'

'The last relationship I had was four years ago. Since then I've been celibate, would you believe. I've wondered if I might be gay and I tried to find out. I would look at men and see if they aroused any feelings in me at all. Sometimes I would have a fantasy about a guy who was sitting opposite me on the train. That was it until you came into my life. When Paul showed us those photographs of you, I couldn't get you out of my mind. I wanted to meet you, to touch you, hold you, sleep with

131

you I suppose, I don't know.' Alex looked at Richard rather sheepishly.

'Let's have another drink,' said Richard and went to the bar to order two more pints. It also gave him time to think. When he got back he said to Alex, 'You could be a bi-sexual, you know. Have you thought of that? If not, then you are probably gay. You could get married and lead a sham of a life or lead separate lives, or you could carry on as you have done for the last four years. I know a guy who's gay and has never had a boyfriend or lover in his life. He is older than us, fifty-five or so, but he couldn't accept the homosexual lifestyle. You also have the choice of finding a boyfriend and setting up home together as long-term partners. The other alternative is to buy your sex. Rent-boys are easy enough to find if you want to. But I would advise you to think carefully and remember that AIDS isn't something that only happens to other people,' lectured Richard.

'I hear what you're saying and I am grateful,' said Alex. 'I wish I'd met you years ago.'

'Something we have all said to someone sometime or another,' said Richard, remembering how he had said just that to Paul. Paul, poor Paul, he hadn't seen much of him in the last couple of days, and he was making even more arrangements to go out.

Alex didn't say any more. He finished his beer and then said he had to go and offered Richard a lift.

'What I have said is confidential, isn't it?' asked Alex again.

'Don't worry, of course it is. I'm better off getting the tube, thanks all the same,' said Richard as they left. 'I'll see you later.'

Chapter 9

It was Saturday and Richard was not required at the studio again until Monday afternoon. In the morning he had his first lesson at acting school. Richard intended to spend every minute of this weekend with Paul. He felt guilty at the way he had neglected Paul lately. He got up and made Paul his breakfast. He knew how much he liked that and it gave them a chance to sit on the bed together. Sometimes they would become intimate. Richard always let Paul make the first move, although Richard was usually the one who finished up without any clothes. Paul would look at Richard for what seemed like hours. Richard found this exciting and when Paul started to touch his body and caress him he was soon in a very erotic state. It was at that stage that Paul called him a slut and threw him out of the room laughing. Richard would retreat to his room to satisfy his libido. He wondered if Paul was doing the same.

Later Richard made Paul a cup of coffee and asked him to sit down for a minute as he had something to say.

'I want to say that I've been a bastard to you this last week. I've been out nearly every night, without giving a thought to how you might feel, or whether you had made any other arrangements. I want to say that I'm sorry, I'll try to be more considerate in the future,' said Richard.

'Is that what's been bothering you? Well it needn't. I don't expect you to ask my permission to go out with your new friends. We're sharing a house as friends, we're not lovers. I don't have any hold over you,' said Paul.

'I knew that was what you'd say. I still feel rotten though. It's just that . . . well, I've never been in a position like this before. I've been for a drink with people who like me for what I am and want a drink with me. All right, I suspect that Michael may have an ulterior motive, and perhaps Alex too. But I don't think either of them want to get me into bed. Practically everybody that I've met since I came to London has finished up in my bed and paying me money. I suddenly feel it's my choice if I want to sleep with them or not. I'm just like most gays now, not like a whore,' said Richard. 'I've never had friends, only other rent-boys, we stuck together for protection. It's a new experience for me, and I'm still learning how to behave. I'm so naive in so many ways and yet so experienced when it comes to sex. When I was with Alex in the pub on Friday he was pouring his heart out to me as if I were the expert; he's at least five years older than me. I had to restrain myself from acting like a whore and taking him outside to the alley. I know what he wants, but it's for him to realise it,' said Richard, looking at Paul to see if he understood that he was finding his new life a bit restrictive.

'I know how you feel, and if you want to find a friend to go with at some time then that's down to you, as we've always said. I'm only too pleased that things are working out for you and that I still have you to look at in the morning and to hug and kiss now and again. If you want my advice, take your time with these people. Let them get to know you and you get to know them. As you so rightly said, you don't have to go to bed with them on the first night. You want to bring Michael back to dinner one night next week, is that right?' asked Paul.

'Yes, if that is OK with you,' said Richard.

'Of course it is. Do you want me to be here or shall I go to the theatre or something?' said Paul.

'No, I want Michael to meet you. I've told him all about you and I've told him we're just friends. He's looking forward to meeting you. I think he's quite lonely.'

'That's fine, when you've fixed the date let me know,' said Paul.

'What shall we do this weekend? Have you got any ideas?' asked Richard.

'Not really, I didn't know what you were doing, so I haven't made any plans. We could go for a drive around Box Hill and Dorking, it's very pretty in that area, and we could stop for lunch somewhere, if you like,' said Paul.

'That sounds great to me. I'll get ready,' said Richard.

'We'll leave in half an hour,' said Paul.

'Fine,' answered Richard.

They drove out to the beautiful Surrey countryside until they found a pub that they both liked the look of and then stopped for lunch. Richard had been uncharacteristically quiet, and although Paul had noticed, he decided not to say anything. If Richard wanted to tell him why he was in such a mood, he would. In the restaurant they ordered their meal, and Richard was still very withdrawn.

'Is there something the matter?' asked Paul. 'You've hardly said a word all day.'

'I'm sorry. I'm not very good company today, am I?' said Richard. 'I've been reviewing the situation, as Fagin said in *Oliver*. I think I can make a go of this. I like acting

135

and I think I'm quite good at it. So they tell me. I like the people that I've met and I'm worried sick that my past life will become public knowledge. I'm also worried about being HIV positive. Doing what I was doing, it almost didn't matter. I wouldn't deliberately pass it on, but if I did, well they all knew the risks of sleeping with a whore, and certainly the guys who were working with me on the movies knew what they were doing. I like Michael and supposing we did get together, safe sex is one thing, but I would have to tell him that I was infected. Then what? Do I have to tell him how I caught it, or do I lie and pretend it was some bloke I met at a club? I'm so confused. Being straight – not a good choice of word – legitimate, is proving to be very hard for me. Can you imagine John keeping me on as his new young actor if he knew that I was HIV positive. And I can imagine what a field day Kate would have! She leads Michael a dog's life for being gay. As I said this morning, it's all so new to me, and I've got to start again on Monday at acting school,' said Richard.

Paul had been watching him but hadn't said a word while Richard was getting this off his chest. Paul had almost forgotten about Richard's HIV test. 'I thought we discussed the possibility that you might go for some counselling. Don't you think it's time that you did something about it? A service like that is entirely confidential and you could tell them all of your worries and explain to them why you're so worried about your new life style,' said Paul.

'Yes, I must make an appointment to see someone, but I'm not so sure about telling them what I used to do and what I'm doing now. The fewer people who know about my past the better,' said Richard. 'Anyway let's forget all that now. Do you want another drink or shall we go?'

'Let's go,' said Paul. 'Promise me that you'll be careful with the guys that you meet, won't you.'

'Of course I will. I'm only talking about Michael and Alex. Alex is not going to suddenly leap out of the closet and want me for a lover, and Michael worships me like a pop star. I think if Michael and I got together it would ruin our relationship for him,' said Richard.

'Well, you know what you're doing,' said Paul.

As they drove home Richard was comparing how he had made movies for Chris and what he was doing for Alex. He made it all sound very dirty and had Paul laughing all the way. Richard really has got a filthy mind, thought Paul.

They had dinner and watched television for a while but neither of them seemed to be able to settle, so they decided to plan a holiday. Richard knew that *Streetcred* would be finished in November, around his twenty-sixth birthday. He had nothing else scheduled after that. If the programme flopped he might never have anything else scheduled.

They looked at some brochures. The Seychelles was always in the back of their minds, but they wanted to see if somewhere else would be as appealing. The Caribbean maybe. They made a list of three islands that they both liked the sound of and some hotels. Paul would visit the travel agent's on Monday.

'Are you sure that you want to go on holiday with me?' asked Paul.

'Of course. Who else would I go away with?' said Richard.

'It's just that I'm old enough to be your father, people are bound to talk,' said Paul.

'I don't care, let them. We're good together Paul. We know that we get on well. We don't get on each other's

137

nerves. We like the same things, and we don't have to be continually displaying our masculinity. We're special, you and I, you know that,' said Richard.

Paul laughed, but wondered; there were still two months to November, would Richard feel the same then?

Monday morning and Richard started acting school. He was expected and everybody knew who he was. The guy who had never acted before and had landed a starring part based on his looks and one screen test. They didn't like him. This was certainly a new experience for Richard. Normally everybody liked him. He tried all he knew to win them over, he smiled, he was humble, he kept a low profile and spoke only when spoken to. Nothing seemed to endear him to the other students. They all tried to show him up, to make him look stupid. Richard thought fuck 'em, what do I care. I'm here to learn. He studied hard and listened to everything he was told about timing, voice projection, speech and accents. In their studies the students did a lot of role playing. Richard didn't push himself forward and was usually the last member to be picked for any team. Bullying at Barnbury, his old school, flashed through his mind. The teacher was watching what was going on and wondered how long Richard would put up with it. He didn't have to put up with it for too long. It soon became apparent to the other students that Richard did have something that they didn't. He could act. His experience in *Streetcred* had helped him a lot, and soon he was making some of the students look like village-hall amateurs. He could tell that he was gradually winning them over and he was pleased that it was his ability that had finally won the day. He started to relax and become his usual happy-go-lucky self. He had always

138

found it easy to talk to people and he had a natural warmth which allowed him to get close to those he knew and worked with. When he had worked for Chris he had found that some of the guys were shy and nervous performing in front of the camera. Richard had always been able to calm those newcomers. He helped them relax by not being too extrovert himself. He hoped that the actors from the drama school would eventually like him too.

Between acting school and *Streetcred* he had little time for fun and soon Richard was beginning to feel like a monk. He had had dinner with Michael and Michael had enjoyed the return evening with Paul and Richard. Paul and Michael hit it off straight away. They talked about the theatre and plays that they had seen. Richard was not as keen on the theatre as Paul and often when Paul went out he went alone. Richard had been right about Michael. He did not want an affair with Richard or anything deeper. He idolised Richard and was only too happy to be with him. They did have sex once. Richard was very careful and made sure that there was no way Michael could have been infected with HIV. Michael had enjoyed it but said that they must never do it again – he liked to think of Richard as someone special. Richard was happy with this and never bothered Michael again. They often went for a drink together and sometimes out for a meal. Michael came back to dinner with Richard and Paul on a number of occasions.

Alex had been very straight with him since they had had that drink, particularly in public. In private Alex was a bit more relaxed and would sometimes joke and camp it up a bit. Richard stayed well clear. He had seen this happen before. When Alex finally accepted that he was gay and did spend the night with someone he would then

139

go at it like a rabbit. For a time he would be the most promiscuous homosexual around. Richard wanted no part of it.

Chapter 10

Streetcred was a hit. Richard Carter was the hottest thing on television. John Simmonds was looking for a script for Richard to make a tv movie. Richard, in the meantime, was still living on cloud nine. He couldn't believe what had happened to him in the last year. He was still living with Paul, although they had talked about Richard getting a place of his own. Richard was happy with Paul. Paul was a friend, almost a good luck charm. Richard's life and luck had changed when he met Paul on holiday. Richard's sex life had been dramatically curtailed with his new life style, with Paul he had all the physical love he needed. He surprised himself. They were like two brothers, or a father and son. Almost!

Richard went out with some of the boys from work to discos and to clubs now and again. He still went for a drink with Michael and even Alex. Other than that he spent most of his time working. One night he had arranged to go to a gay club with two guys from the studio, Mark and Phil. It wasn't the first time that they had been out together and they got on pretty well. They went for a couple of drinks and then to the club. As they walked through the door Richard spotted a guy coming out of the cloakroom. He had not slept with anybody for nearly a year because he did not want to take the risk of giving any partner AIDS. He had restrained himself and kept in control until now. But this guy he wanted. He couldn't take his eyes from him. He was about the same height as Richard and had blond hair, a good body and sex appeal, at least as far as Richard was concerned. Suddenly Richard realised that he had been staring at the guy, and that the guy had been staring at him. Richard walked over to him.

'Hi, like what you see?' Richard said, using some of his previous work lines.

'Sorry. Was I staring?' said the guy in an Australian accent. 'It's just that I know you and I was trying to place you. You're Richard Carter from *Streetcred*, aren't you?'

'Yes. I didn't know I was so famous,' grinned Richard.

'I'm surprised to see you in a gay club, what would your fans say? Or are you just visiting to get experience for a part? That's what they usually say, isn't it?' asked the Australian.

'No, I'm gay and I've never tried to hide it. I don't go around flaunting it either,' said Richard. 'Can I buy you a drink?'

'Sure, never say no to a tinny,' he said. 'My name's Todd, do I call you Dick?'

'Not if you value your life, you don't,' answered Richard. 'Richard will do.'

'How long have your been acting, only you don't seem to be too clued up on public appearances,' asked Todd.

'*Streetcred* was my first job, I've been at it now for about a year.'

'What were you doing before that?'

Richard knew that that would be the next question. 'I

142

used to do some modelling and photographic work for catalogues, that sort of thing.'

'Hey, that's what I used to do back home, pose for pictures,' said Todd.

There was something in the way that he said it which made Richard think that the pictures he posed for were not likely to appear in a catalogue. He didn't care. Richard was already lusting after this boy.

'Do you want to stay here? Come back to my place, I'm sure we could have some fun. If you have to go to work tomorrow I could always run you into town,' invited Richard.

'Screw work,' said Todd. 'Let's go, I'd like a bit of fun with you.' Todd was grinning and seemed a lot happier now that he had scored.

Richard felt scared. He was being forcefully reminded of his past and he didn't like it. He realised how much he missed the sexual escape he had enjoyed as a rent-boy. He kept looking at Todd from the corner of his eye. He really fancied him. Something about him turned Richard on. He remembered what Todd had said about fans seeing him in a gay club. He hadn't thought his notoriety would affect his private life. He would have to be more careful in the future. He hoped that Paul was in bed when they got home. He didn't want Paul to know about Todd, not yet. What was he going to tell Paul if he decided to move in with Todd. Perhaps that would never happen. Todd might just be looking for a one-night stand, particularly if that person was semi-famous. This was all flashing through Richard's jumbled mind as they drove to Hounslow.

Richard opened the door, relieved to see that all the lights were off. Paul was in bed. Richard led Todd to his

143

room. They started to make love passionately. Richard stopped.

'We can't carry on like this. I've got AIDS.'

Todd stopped, looked at Richard and said, 'are you sure?'

'Yes. At least, I'm HIV positive,' said Richard.

'I'm impressed that you told me. Most guys wouldn't have bothered until afterwards,' said Todd.

'I got caught by someone who knew that he was infected and didn't say anything. I don't want that to happen to anyone I sleep with,' said Richard. 'This doesn't mean we have to go straight to sleep,' he grinned. 'I'm sure we can think of some things we could do. Come here,' Todd rolled over towards him.

The next morning Richard awoke and for the moment forgot that somebody else would be in his bed. It had been so long. He looked at Todd and thought, I must find out more about this boy because I think I'm falling in love with him. What am I going to tell Paul?

Todd was awake and was looking around the room. He noticed the fine furniture and the expensive bed linen, the tasteful wallpaper and decorations.

'Good morning,' he said stroking Richard's arm. 'It was good last night and I'd like to think it was more than a one-night stand. Can we see each other again?' asked Todd.

'I don't know. I hope so, but it's very complicated. Suffice it to say that this is not my house. It belongs to a friend, Paul, who's sleeping in the next room. I need to explain about you to Paul and I need to tell you about him. When you understand that Paul will always come first with me, then we have got the grounds for a permanent relationship. I'm not trying to give you the brushoff, I really would like us to become a partnership. The best thing now is for you to go so that I can talk to Paul and I'll see you tonight. What do you say?' asked Richard.

'I'm thoroughly intrigued. I'll meet you tonight in the pub on the corner by the club where we met – at about seven-thirty. OK?' said Todd.

'Yes, now you'd better go.'

Todd got dressed and Richard showed him out.

'Good morning.' Paul was standing behind him. Richard turned and knew from the expression on Paul's face that he was not pleased.

'Paul. Can we talk?'

'I think we had better. I don't like you bringing your pick-ups back to my house, Richard, particularly without my permission, and then trying to smuggle them out before I get up,' said Paul. 'I'm so angry. I've been good to you, Richard and I think I deserve better than that. I almost feel like throwing you out.'

'Please, Paul, let me try to explain. I know that I shouldn't have asked Todd to come back here last night. It was unforgivable, but he said something that made me panic and I reverted to acting like a rent-boy. He recognised me from *Streetcred* and said he was surprised to see me in a gay club. What would my fans say? I'd never thought of it like that. I wanted to leave, but I didn't want to leave Todd. We were getting on well and I liked him. An understatement. I know this is sudden, but do you remember saying to me that if I found someone nearer my own age you wouldn't stand in my way if I wanted to live with him? I'm afraid the day has arrived. Todd and I developed a good rapport and as he's an active gay he was driving me crazy. I wanted him. I've been celibate now for a year and it can't go on. Paul, I want to find a place of my own and move in with Todd. I want him in my bed at night. What I don't want is to upset or lose

145

you. I want our relationship to remain as it has been for the last year, perhaps even growing stronger. I've told Todd that you will always be first with me. I'm seeing him tonight and I'm going to ask him to share my life. That means that I'd like him to meet you, and for you two to be friends.'

'I doubt if we could be that,' said Paul. 'Is it just sex? If I agreed for us to make love, would you forget Todd?' asked Paul.

'I could never let you do that and you know it, Paul. Meet Todd, maybe you'll like him,' begged Richard.

'I'll meet him, but I'm not promising anything,' said Paul. 'I know that I'm being selfish, but I can't help it. I've been so happy with you living here, it has put new life into me. I like Michael coming round now and again, I'll miss it all. Yes, you have my blessing, and don't forget, you're always welcome here any time, day or night.'

'Paul, I love you,' said Richard jumping up to give Paul a kiss and hug. Richard's eyes were beginning to fill with tears.

'Oh, for Christ's sake, don't start crying, I couldn't stand that at this time of the morning.' Paul put his arms round Richard and said, 'I suppose that deep down I knew that this day would come. I still want to see you. If you must bring Todd, OK, but sometimes I want to see you on your own. After all, I don't just want to rely on my memory of how your body looks,' grinned Paul.

'You mean like this,' Richard dropped his dressing gown and posed for Paul as he knew he liked.

'Put your clothes on, you tart,' laughed Paul.

They decided to eat lunch out and where better than the pub by the river that they had been to so long ago, on

146

that first weekend. So much had happened. Paul was now his old self and was quite cheery. Richard was still a little depressed. Paul had been the only friend he had had in his twenty-six years, and somehow he felt he was letting him down. He knew already that he had to try to make a life for himself and Todd, if for no other reason than to release some of the pent-up passion he had for him. If he ignored it he knew that he would finish by blaming Paul. That must never happen.

Paul bought Richard another pint. 'Come on, this isn't a wake. Cheer up. I'll be able to keep you as a mistress, something I've always wanted,' laughed Paul. His life had changed completely because he had met a boy at an airport. It was still hard to believe.

'Where are you going to live until you find a place, are you moving in with Todd?' asked Paul.

'No, I can't. He shares with three other blokes. One's gay and the other two are straight. There isn't enough room,' said Richard.

'You could stay with me if you like. It will give me a chance to get to know Todd. I hate to keep on, but are you sure that you're doing the right thing? You don't seem to know a lot about him, apart from the size of his genitals. Do you know his surname or where he works? He stopped. 'I'm sorry, I won't mention it again,' said Paul.

'Can we really stay with you, Paul? That would be marvellous,' said Richard. 'But I know you, Paul Green, you still have a lot more to say. Please say it and let's clear the air.'

'I can't help wondering, has he got another boyfriend? You said he shares with one gay and two straights. Perhaps he is sharing more than you thought with this gay. Maybe he was star-struck and is now telling everybody that he's slept with Richard Carter, the star of *Streetcred*,' said Paul.

Richard went white. 'Do you really think he's telling people that?' he said. 'I didn't think. I was so taken in by his looks and body all I wanted was to get him into my bed.'

'I know what you mean,' said Paul wistfully.

'Do you really think I might be making a mistake, Paul? You wouldn't say this just to . . .'

'Just to what?' asked Paul. 'Just so that you wouldn't leave me. Richard, you know me better than that.'

'Yes, I know. I'm sorry. I shouldn't have said that. I know you wouldn't. You're right, though. I don't know much about him. I'll take it a lot slower tonight and find out a lot more about him before I start making commitments. Could I bring him back anyway? I'd like you to meet him and see what you think,' said Richard.

'Good idea, he's seen the house. He may think that you're loaded,' said Paul.

'He knows that already,' grinned Richard.

'You know what I mean. Can't you think of anything else but sex?'

'Not if I can help it,' said Richard.

'What am I going to do with you?'

'Do you want me to make a few suggestions?'

They were both laughing. It was a good job no one else was sitting near enough to hear this conversation.

Richard left saying that he would see Paul later and made his way to the pub where he had made arrangements to meet Todd. He arrived at about seven-thirty, not too late, not too early. He went in and looked around to see if he could see Todd. No sign of him. He hated this sort of gay bar. All very feminine, a lot of posing. He had a feeling that he should get out of there as soon as possible. He turned to go just as Todd walked in.

'Come on, let's get out of this dump,' said Richard.

'Hi, Todd, how are you, Todd. Nice to see you again. I've been thinking about you all day,' said Todd.

'All right. Hi, Todd. How are you and I *have* been thinking about you today and it usually made me horny. Now, can we get out of this dump?' said Richard.

'Yes, I agree it's not very nice, particularly for someone like you.'

'What do you mean?' asked Richard, noticing for the first time a sarcastic streak in Todd.

'Nothing, but you *are* famous,' said Todd.

'Is that what you like about me? Have you told your flatmates that you slept with the star of *Streetcred*?' asked Richard.

'No, of course not. I want you all to myself,' said Todd.

'Where are we going?'

'Back to my place. Paul wants to meet you, and I think we should find out more about each other.'

'This Paul seems to have a hold over you – who is he?' asked Todd.

'It's not like that at all. Paul and I are very good friends, as I've told you. I would never hurt him and he'd never let me get hurt. I don't know much about you – where you live, your surname, where you work or what you do. I thought if we're going to get together it might be nice to have dinner with Paul and we can all get to know each other,' said Richard.

'Sounds great to me. I get a free meal out of it,' said Todd.

'Well, what is your surname, then at least I can introduce you properly?' asked Richard.

'My surname is Jones. Very ordinary isn't it. I'm twen-

149

ty-three, I'm an Australian. What else do you want to know?'

'Nothing, get in the car, let's drive.'

It took about forty-five minutes to get to Paul's house. Richard introduced Todd to Paul and Paul poured them some drinks.

'Dinner won't be long, I didn't get everything ready until you got here, as I know what Richard is. If the fancy takes him he'll stay out all night,' said Paul.

'Thanks for the character reference,' said Richard. 'You see what I have to put up with.'

'It's nice that someone cares about you. Where did you meet Richard, Paul? He hasn't told me anything,' said Todd.

'We met on holiday last year. We got on really well and have been close friends since,' said Paul. 'Only friends – I'm not sure that I could cope with Richard's appetites, I'm too old.' He winked at Todd.

'I know what you mean, Richard and I got it on together straight away. There was a certain amount of electricity between us immediately,' said Todd, 'But I'm not trying to take advantage of him.'

I wonder what he meant by that, Paul thought. He turned to Richard, but he was gazing at Todd as if he couldn't wait to get him in bed.

'How long is it since you left Australia?' asked Paul.

'About three years now. I stopped off in Bangkok and Hong Kong before coming to England,' answered Todd.

'What were you doing back home, wherever that was? Where, in Australia do you come from?' asked Richard.

Todd was beginning to dislike this inquisition, certainly when Richard took part. He had expected it from the old guy.

'I originally came from Sydney, but I've lived all over.

150

I'm a mechanic really, but I can turn my hand to anything. You have to when you're moving around as much as I do,' said Todd.

'You sound a bit of a drifter,' said Paul. 'Don't you want to settle down in one place for a while.'

'Oh yes, I do now. I want to settle in London. I like it here and I've met some good blokes,' said Todd.

'What made you want to leave the sun, sea and sand for the cold weather of England. Do you have any family in England?' said Paul.

'No. We go back for generations in Australia,' said Todd.

'Did you have a boyfriend at home?' said Richard.

'No, not a regular one. You're the first person that I have wanted to live with,' said Todd.

Paul didn't believe that for one minute. In fact he felt that a lot of what Todd said was either for effect or was a downright lie. He could see that Richard was besotted with him and it would make no difference if he said as much to him. Amazing, when he thought of the life Richard had led.

'Todd, Paul and I have spoken about this, and he is agreeable for you to move in with me here until I can get us a flat. It shouldn't be for too long. What do you say? Will you live with me?' asked Richard. 'You know that I'm crazy about you.'

Crazy is right, thought Paul.

'Sounds great to me. I'll get my things tomorrow. If you're working I could get a taxi to take me home and bring me back. I haven't got a lot, but too much to carry on the tube,' said Todd, grinning from ear to ear.

'As a matter of fact I am working tomorrow,' said Richard.

151

'The only thing is I don't get paid until Friday, could you lend me thirty pounds for the fare. I'll pay you back.'
'Of course,' said Richard.
Paul said nothing.

Chapter 11

Richard found a flat within three days. He and Todd moved from Paul's and settled down together for what proved to be a very stormy relationship. The sex was good, even with the restraints Richard placed on them. After all, Richard had enough experience to make a randy young Australian happy without repeating a move. However, Todd didn't like work, and as soon as he moved in with Richard he quit his job. With that went his only source of income. He was constantly asking for money. It was always the same story. 'You want me to look nice when I'm with you, don't you, and I'll pay you back.' Richard never saw a penny. He was still infatuated with the boy, he hardly ever went to see Paul, but he did telephone. He didn't want to see Paul because he knew what he would say about Todd, and he knew that he would be right. Todd wanted to be out every night at gay bars and clubs. Richard didn't like this. It made him nervous. He had a fear of an exposé in the tabloids. Apart from anything else Richard was tired; he was up early in the morning, and working hard and long hours. He was not spending as much time with Todd, who was soon complaining that he was being ignored and that if Richard didn't show him some more consideration he would invite a few friends of his own around.

Richard finished a shoot early one day and, as he was not required for the next day either, he went straight home. When he walked into the living room what he saw threw him into a rage the like of which Todd had never seen before. He told Todd to get out immediately. He went to their room and packed his things into his back-pack and bodily ushered him out of the flat.

Richard sat down and realised, not for the first time, what a fool he'd been. He picked up the phone and rang Paul.

'Can I come home?' he asked.

'Do you need to ask?' said Paul.

Richard packed his things and locked the flat. He didn't want to stay in that place ever again. He would hand in the keys in the morning, even if it did mean losing his deposit.

He arrived at Hounslow at eight o'clock. Paul had poured him a drink, which he readily accepted.

'Get it off your chest, I can tell you're really mad,' said Paul.

'What makes me so mad is that I'm such a fucking idiot. I'm sorry, but I've been such a fool. You knew that Todd was a load of rubbish, didn't you?' said Richard.

'Yes,' said Paul.

'Why did you let me go with him?' asked Richard.

'Would you have listened to anything I said at the time? I'm only too glad that it didn't take any longer than it did for you to realise what a fool he was making of you,' said Paul. 'You were blind to the faults that boy had. All you could see was the sex. You had to get him out of your system. Do you want to tell me what happened?'

'I got home early. As I opened the door I couldn't

154

believe the mess. Beer cans everywhere, the smell of can-
nabis was so strong it almost made me gag. And you
know my views on any drugs. Four guys, including Todd,
were partying like you've never seen. I'm not easily
shocked, not with my background, but this was disgusting. The fruits of their afternoon's play were all over the
floor and furniture. I was so angry. I threw him and his
mates out. He's had money from me ever since we moved
into the flat; he's been using me since the first time we
met and he knew who I was. I let him talk me into going
to gay bars and clubs. If it gets back to John or Alex,
they'll be furious. I'm exhausted, I think I'll go to bed, if
you don't mind. Please Paul, don't let me do anything
daft like this again. You have my permission to knock the
shit out of me if necessary. Good night.'

The next morning Richard was a lot calmer. He had
decided to spend as much time as possible with Paul. He
had hardly seen him in weeks. Richard made breakfast
and took it to Paul's room.

'Good morning, how are you this morning?' asked
Richard.

'I'm fine now that you're home,' said Paul.

'I'm sorry, Paul. I've been a prat again and behaved
badly towards you. I've hardly seen you,' said Richard.

'You know what your trouble is, don't you? What's
between your legs rules your head and your heart. Stop
reacting with this one-night-stand mentality. Try to get
to know the men that you go out with. Don't think you
have to bed them the first time you meet them. I'm surprised that at the press events and at the studio you
haven't met someone already. You must realise that if a
guy has a good job or he's in the public eye he's going to
be discreet. He is not going to camp it up, any approach

155

will be subtle. Although I have never taken up the offers, the advances have been there,' said Paul.

'You're a wise old bird, aren't you?' said Richard. 'I've met a few people I think are gay, some I know are, and I have been out with them a few times, to discos and to clubs. You're right, though. I must start thinking with my head and not my cock in future,' said Richard.

'I take it you're not working today. What do you want to do, how about booking a flight to Mahé? If we're able to book a suitable flight then we could see what sort of hotel accommodation we could find around the islands. What do you think?' asked Paul.

'I think it sounds great. I'm due some time off when this series ends,' said Richard, delighted.

Richard phoned the office and asked if he could take some time off when *Streetcred* was finished. Dates were agreed on the understanding that flights were available. He told Paul and said he would be ready to go in ten minutes.

Paul got the car from the garage and they drove to the travel agent's.

They booked a flight on Air Seychelles and made arrangements to stay at Beau Vallon until the Tuesday. The next stop was to be La Digue, where they booked to stay at the Island Lodge for a week and then a few days on Frigate, a week on Praslin, staying at La Reserve, and finally a couple of days on Mahé before returning to England.

When everything was confirmed Richard suggested that they call in to the studio to confirm it with Sally. Sally co-ordinated all travel arrangements to avoid any clashes with production schedules.

They were walking through reception when the receptionist called to Richard. 'Mr Carter, a letter arrived for

156

you by hand a little while ago. I told the gentleman that you were not in today, and he asked for your private address. I told him that we were not allowed to pass on private information. He asked if you would be in tomorrow. I checked and told him that you were expected. He then decided to leave the letter, saying that it was urgent.'

'Thank you,' said Richard, flashing a dazzling smile at the girl. 'The man didn't leave his name, did he, Ellen?'

'No, sir,' she answered.

'Not to worry,' said Richard.

Paul laughed to himself as he watched this young girl almost pass out as she was talking to Richard. I bet that story is relayed to her girl friends more than once. Richard put the letter in his pocket and carried on down the corridor to book his holiday with Sally.

They bumped into Alex Smith on their way out and he asked Paul and Richard to lunch. It wasn't until he got home that night that Richard remembered the letter. He was quite surprised to find that it was from Chris. He read the letter and the blood drained from his face.

'What on earth is the matter?' asked Paul. 'You look terrible.'

'It's from Chris,' said Richard.

'Is he trying to cause trouble?' asked Paul.

'No, I told you Chris isn't like that. We're friends. Read it,' said Richard, handing the letter to Paul.

Paul read the letter and then understood why Richard had gone so white. Chris had written to say that he had been burgled the day before and after turning the place upside down the thief had taken only one thing: a copy of a video that Richard had made. Chris wanted to see Richard to talk. He had not informed the police yet, as the only thing missing was the tape.

Paul looked at Richard who was still a bit shaken, but was beginning to show signs of anger.

'What shall I do, Paul? I think I should see Chris as soon as possible, don't you?'

'Yes, I do,' said Paul.

'It's what I was afraid might happen. If this gets back to the studio . . . what then? Damn Chris. He said he hadn't got any copies, that every one of the copies were sold in Germany or Holland. He could ruin everything,' said Richard.

'Calm down. Don't you think you're being a bit hard on Chris? He's allowed to keep whatever he likes in his private video collection. He need not have bothered to tell you. After all, nothing else was taken,' said Paul. 'I think you should phone Chris and invite him over and we can talk about it.'

'I would like to know who else knew that he had that tape,' said Richard.

'Who else have you told about your dealings with Chris?' asked Paul.

'Nobody,' said Richard.

'Not even Todd? He seemed like the sort of person that could worm all sorts of tit-bits out of you,' asked Paul.

'No, I don't think so,' said Richard.

'Fair enough, why don't you ring Chris and we can hear what he has to say,' said Paul.

Richard telephoned. Chris was in and he seemed pleased to be invited to dinner. He said he would be there by eight.

Paul and Richard prepared dinner and had drinks ready when Chris arrived.

'Chris, it's good to see you again. How are you? Are the boys behaving themselves?' smiled Richard.

158

'Yes, everything is fine, or at least it was until the burglary. I'm sorry, Richard, I feel responsible. If I hadn't kept a copy it couldn't have happened. It was just that you were so good I had to have some memento,' explained Chris as he was shaking Richard's hand.

'Chris, I would like to introduce you to Paul. Paul is the man I left the underworld of porn for. Paul, this is Chris, an old friend of mine.'

Paul and Chris shook hands and eyed each other like animals, each wondering what the other had done to their boy.

'How do you do,' said Paul. 'Richard has told me a lot about you and always rates you as a friend.'

'Thanks. Richard has told me a lot about you too. All good. I just wish that I had sent him home all those years ago. He wouldn't be in this mess now if I had,' said Chris.

'Let's hope that between us we can sort it out,' said Paul.

'Do you two mind, I *am* standing here, you know, and I do have a mind of my own and I did at sixteen too. If you had sent me home, Chris, I'd never have met Paul,' said Richard, putting his arm around Paul's shoulder.

'If he gets out of line give him a good slapping,' said Chris to Paul with a grin.

'He does,' said Richard.

'Dinner's ready, let's eat. We can continue this conversation over the meal,' said Paul.

'Tell us what happened, Chris. Have you any idea who did it, and why should they steal only a copy of my film?' said Richard anxiously.

Paul looked at Chris. He could see that he knew why a burglar would take only a copy of Richard's film.

'Richard, I think we have a problem on our hands. As the thief took only your tape that must have been what

159

he was looking for. If that's the case we must think about why he took it. I think that someone has found out that Richard Carter is Dick Hard, and wants to see what the newspapers would pay for proof. I'm sorry to break it to you like that, but I think I'm right, don't you Chris?' asked Paul.

'Unfortunately, yes I do. That's why I wanted to get in touch with you as soon as possible. Have you got any idea who could have found out about your past? I haven't told anybody, and the guys at the studio aren't going to say anything. You know most of them don't want it known what they're doing.'

'No, I've got no idea,' said Richard, looking a bit stunned. 'I can't believe this is happening, not when things were going so well. It's not fair.'

'You've got no idea then, Richard?' said Chris.

'No, I've said that, haven't I?' shouted Richard. 'If you hadn't kept a copy, this wouldn't have happened!'

'I think you owe Chris an apology,' said Paul. 'It's no use trying to blame someone who's trying to help. We've got to think who knew or could have found out about your past.'

'I'm sorry Chris, it's just my big mouth again,' apologised Richard.

'What about Michael, have you said anything to him? Todd Jones still seems the most likely candidate. Richard, think. Did you ever mention to him what you used to do? After all, when you two were in bed he must have realised that you were pretty experienced and had picked up that knowledge somewhere,' said Paul.

'Todd Jones,' said Chris, 'do you know him?'

'I lived with him for a while,' said Richard.

'I think we've found our connection,' said Chris. 'Todd came to me for work in the movies. I tried him out but

160

he was a sadist – and worse. I wouldn't employ him. If he discovered that you even knew me he would be able to put two and two together.'

'I probably spoke of you as a friend, but I'm sure that I didn't mention even working for you, let alone what I did,' said Richard.

'He would have drawn his own conclusions,' said Chris.

'I knew that guy would cause trouble. What do we do now? We don't know for sure that he did take the tape, but if he did, how do we go about getting it back?' mused Paul. 'Do you want to go to the police, Chris?'

'Not if I can help it. I will though, if it'll do any good.'

'I think I have an idea,' said Richard. 'I know where Todd lives. I could go to see him. He's greedy by nature; if I offered him money and my body – he always liked that – I might be able to persuade him to give me the tape. What do you think?'

'I think it's a ridiculous idea. You're not a rent-boy now – you can't go offering your body to people as if it were a commodity on the open market. Todd is greedy. I think we have got to work along those lines to persuade him to return the tape,' said Paul. 'But how?'

Chris said, 'I think the first thing to do is to establish that Todd has got the tape, and then what he intends to do with it. You're going to have to go to see him, Richard, and confront him with our suspicions. Do you agree, Paul?'

'Yes, I think that's the first step. You'll have to be careful, Richard. Todd is a nasty character and he might turn violent,' said Paul.

'Don't worry about that. I can take care of myself and I can certainly take care of a slimy little creep like him. Remember, I was on the streets for a good few years. You have to be able to look after yourself or you wouldn't survive very long. Isn't that right, Chris?' said Richard.

'I think you know how to handle Todd Jones. Nevertheless, Paul is right – take care. We're not talking about one client more or less; this could be big money to Todd and if he has found himself a partner . . . well, it might get heavy,' said Chris.

'OK, OK, I'll be a good boy. What shall I say to him? I think you've got a tape of me which you stole from Chris and I want it back. He's just going to laugh,' said Richard.

'Tomorrow morning phone him and say that you want to see him. You've found out that he knew who you were working for before your acting career. A friend has been burgled and a tape has gone missing. You are prepared to pay to have it returned. Watch for his reactions all the time, you'll have to rely on your own instinct. If he looks completely baffled, maybe we have got the wrong man. My guess is that he'll want to know how much you're willing to pay. Don't give him a figure – make him believe that you'll pay anything. Find out where the tape is. He may not have it now. He may already have sold it to someone else, maybe the newspapers. He could have given it to somebody he trusts to keep safe for him. They wouldn't need to know what was in the parcel. If you can make him show you the tape, so much the better. Get hold of it and keep hold of it,' said Paul. 'If he's sold it on, you must find out to whom. If the trail stops at Todd we won't have a chance in hell of getting it back.'

'Sounds good to me,' said Chris. 'What do you think, Richard?'

'I don't think I have any choice. If that tape goes onto the open market or if any pictures are published in the newspaper, I'm dead. I'll never get another straight job, and no one is going to want to touch me on the streets when it's known that I was a porno actor. They'll all think that I have AIDS. Which, of course, I have,' said Richard, despondently.

'There's nothing else we can do tonight. I suggest we have another drink and then sleep on it,' said Paul.

'I'll skip the drink, if you don't mind', said Chris. 'I've got the car. It's been a very good evening, Paul. Thank you for your hospitality and it's a pity we didn't meet under happier circumstances. Take care of my boy.'

'Thanks, Chris. Of course I'll take care of him,' said Paul, putting his arm around Richard's shoulder. 'I have a feeling, though, that he's very capable of looking after himself on this one and the less I know about the details the better.'

'He hasn't kept that body and those looks by accident: no scars, no flat nose. He's a tough bastard when he gets riled,' said Chris.

'You're doing it again. I am here you know. Talking about me as if I was in another room,' said Richard, indignantly.

Chris kissed him and said, 'Shut up'.

Paul and Richard watched Chris drive off. 'Quite a night,' said Paul.

'Yes,' said Richard. 'But tomorrow I'm going to be fighting for my life and I don't intend to lose. Todd Jones didn't know what he was taking on when he picked on me. I'm not his infatuated lover now.'

The next morning Richard drove to Todd's flat. He knocked at the door and waited for an answer. The door opened. It was Todd. He looked surprised.

'Well, if it isn't Mr Goody Goody! What do you want?' asked Todd.

'Can I come in? I think what I've got to say might be better said in private,' said Richard.

Todd ushered Richard in and shut the door behind him.

'Well, what do you want?' said Todd 'I thought you never wanted to see a sadist and pervert like me ever again. Wasn't that what you said?'

'Yes, that is what I said and I still mean it, but I believe that you've been misbehaving yourself and have removed from his possession a tape belonging to a friend of mine which he would like back.' Richard was staring into Todd's eyes all the time he was talking and there was no doubt that the Australian understood what Richard was saying. One hurdle over, thought Richard. At least Todd did take the tape.

'What makes you think I've got this tape? Why would I want a tape of you?' said Todd.

'Did I say that was what the tape was about? I don't remember that,' said Richard. 'Still, you are right and I want it back. Are you going to give it to me, or are you going to make things difficult?'

'If you want the tape you've got to find it first and I'm not going to be of any help,' sneered Todd.

'Oh, aren't you,' said Richard giving Todd the full force of his knee in the groin. 'Don't play with me, Todd. I can be extremely nasty if I like.'

Todd was down on his knees holding his balls. He did not look too well.

'I haven't got the tape, any tape!' he cried.

'I told you, don't mess me about.' Richard gave Todd another kicking and slapped his face. 'I want that tape now. The longer you play silly buggers the more you'll get hurt. I'm not having the best thing that has ever happened to me ruined, particularly by a creep like you.

Now where is it and do I get it, or do you want me to really start hitting you? Because I will, you know that, don't you?'

'I haven't got it,' screamed Todd. He was well aware that Richard would hit him again and again. 'I sent it to the newspapers.'

'You did what?' said Richard horrified. 'When? Which paper? Why?'

'I wanted money and I knew that they'd pay for something as hot as that,' said Todd.

'You're a bigger fool than I took you for. Don't you realise that it will be almost impossible for them to publish any of the tape. Didn't it occur to you that I might have paid you money for its return?' said Richard.

'Oh, I think they'll publish the tape all right,' said Todd, feeling a lot more confident now. 'I also gave them the lowdown on our stormy time together. I also told them how I left you when I got home unexpectedly to find you in an orgy with three other men.'

'Why, you lying bastard. I'll kill you!' Richard reached for Todd and pulled him to his feet. He started to hit him and his temper went totally out of control. He smashed his fist into Todd's face and his stomach over and over again. He stopped when he could see that Todd wasn't resisting at all. What the hell have I done? He felt his pulse and listened for his breathing. He was alive. Which was more than he deserved. Richard was in control now, he had calmed down. I must find out if it's true he has sent the tape to the press. If he has, to whom? Richard started to search the flat looking for something that might tell him which newspaper had the tape. After ten minutes of extensive searching he found what he had been looking for – a note saying that they would pay Todd two thousand pounds for the sole use of a video tape supplied to

165

them by Todd Jones. The name on the letter was the last name that Richard would have expected to see buying the tape. He left the flat with the receipt after taking one last look at Todd, who was just about beginning to come round.

Richard went back to his car. He set off towards home, but he started shaking so much he had to stop. After a while he felt better, but decided to go to the studio to see Chris rather than go home to Paul.

Richard arrived at the studio and asked at the reception if he could see Chris as it was urgent. He noticed the receptionist staring at him and he realised he must look a mess. He had probably broken Todd's nose and he had certainly cut his lip. He looked at himself; he had blood on his clothes and on his hands.

'Been in a bit of an accident,' he said. Chris came through. When he saw Richard he told the girl to cancel all his appointments for the day and dragged Richard into his private studio where he knew that they wouldn't be disturbed.

'Tell me what the hell has been going on. I thought you were going to talk to Todd, not beat him to death, which is what it looks like. You haven't, have you?' asked Chris with a worried expression on his face.

'No, he was all right when I left, but do you know what he did?' said Richard.

Richard proceeded to tell Chris all the details of that morning's visit to Todd's flat. Finally he showed him the receipt.

'Why on earth did he go to them? The tabloids would have jumped at the chance to play with scandal like this,' said Chris.

'I know, that's what I thought. It does put a different complexion on things though, doesn't it?' said Richard.

166

'Why?' said Chris.

'A newspaper like that would not print scandal for the sake of it. Why did they buy it? But what is more important is, can I buy it back? I'd like to talk to Paul and give this some thought. The game has changed – somebody has changed the rules in the middle of a hand. Why don't you come over tonight too. I'm sure Paul would be pleased to see you and you are as involved in this as we all are,' said Richard.

'Yes, I think, I will. I'll be there at about eight. Will you tell Paul, or shall I phone him?' said Chris.

'No, I'll tell him. Can I clean myself up a bit and then I must go. Paul will be worried,' said Richard.

'Not without cause,' said Chris. 'You are sure that Todd was all right?'

'Yes, he was OK. I admit I did lose my temper, but he's such a wimp he didn't put up any fight at all. I soon realised that he was unconscious and I stopped hitting him. It was when he said that he had told the papers that I was the one in the orgy performing the perverted acts that in fact he was performing, I snapped. You know, Chris, that I never do anything like that.'

'Yes, I know, kid, and so does Paul. Who else counts? Take it easy driving home and I'll see you later,' said Chris.

'See you later,' said Richard dismally, and left to drive home.

Richard told Paul exactly what had happened at Todd's. He could see that Paul didn't approve of what Richard had done and was quite worried about Todd's condition. Richard explained that Todd was regaining consciousness as he was leaving and that he was trying to get to his feet.

167

'If you say so,' said Paul. 'I'm surprised that a person like you could be so violent. You have a dark side that I've never seen.'

'It's not a side of my character that I'm proud of. It started when I first came to London. Sometimes a client would try to beat up on me, usually for kicks, because I was young. Chris told me I would have to learn to defend myself. He was right, and so I did. Unfortunately, I have a bad temper. The older I've got the easier it's been to control. Except today. What do you think about that paper buying the tape?'

'I think it's the best thing that has happened so far, but let's wait until Chris arrives and then discuss it,' said Paul.

'Are you prepared to go to the newspaper and say that you are the guy in the tape and you would like to have it back? It would leave you wide open to exposure if you admitted it,' said Paul.

'I know, that's why I want to talk it over with you and Chris,' said Richard.

'He should be here soon. Do you want a drink?' said Paul.

'Thanks,' said Richard.

A knock at the front door let them know that Chris had arrived.

After the greetings and drinks had been distributed Chris said to Paul, 'What do you think of our little hot-head?'

'I'm worried that Todd might be badly hurt. I'm also surprised that a guy who I have known as a gentle, caring person has such a violent streak,' said Paul.

'You don't have to worry about Todd. I phoned him after Richard had gone. I made Richard give me his number. Todd is all right, calling Richard all sorts of names, but I don't think he'll take it any farther. He's basically a coward and he doesn't want any more trouble. He's now become acutely aware that Richard is not someone to be messed with,' said Chris. 'In fact, I wouldn't be surprised if Mr Jones decided it was time to move on from London and to see more of Europe.'

'Thank God for that,' said both Paul and Richard.

'Do you think that the paper has an ulterior motive for buying the tape?' It seems so out of character,' asked Paul.

'I don't know, but it does leave us with some more avenues to explore as far as getting the tape back is concerned. Let's examine what can be done next. We could walk in and demand that the tape is returned as it is stolen property, if not we'll call the police. Not a good move. We could ask if they have the tape and what they intend to do with it if they do. Publish? Remember Todd said he also gave them a written statement – what about that? I'm more interested in why they bought it in the first place,' said Chris.

'I agree,' said Richard. 'Are they thinking of doing a feature on pornography? Maybe they bought it to stop the other, less scrupulous papers getting their hands on it and have no intention of publishing anything anyway.'

'An interesting thought, but I can't see a commercial enterprise paying two thousand pounds for a tape that they have no intention of using,' said Paul.

'I think we've got to take the bull by the horns and go to see the editor and face him with it. We've got a receipt saying that he has sole rights to a tape which I know has been stolen and that he may have a written statement that is untrue and could never be proved one way or the other. What does he intend doing with them? Let's see if he's willing to sell them back to us,' said Chris.

169

'I think a meeting with the editor is the first step,' said Paul. 'I think that Richard and I should go to see him as soon as possible. Are we agreed?'

'Yes, I am,' said Chris.

'Good. I'll try to fix an appointment with the said gentleman tomorrow. OK, Richard? Can you get time off work?'

'If we don't get this sorted out I won't have any work,' said Richard. 'Paul, one thing did occur to me. Should I tell the studio – John or Alex – to warn them that something might blow. I could be selective with what I tell them. They've been good to me. I wouldn't want them to suffer unduly because of it,' said Richard.

'I think you should wait until we've seen the editor. It may make a difference to what you say, but in principle, yes,' said Paul.

First thing in the morning Paul telephoned the editor and asked if he could have an appointment as soon as possible to discuss a matter regarding a tape which he had reason to believe was in the newspaper's possession. The editor was on the phone immediately.

'Who are you, and how did you know about that tape?' he asked.

'My name is not important at the moment, but I can assure you that the tape is stolen and I am authorised to get its return,' said Paul. 'I am sure we could talk about this in more privacy in your office. Neither I nor my associates are crooks. We wish only to talk to you and have the tape returned. I'm sure you would not find yourself out of pocket,' said Paul.

'Very well, shall we say two-thirty p.m.? May I have your name?' said the editor.

'My name is Paul Green and I will be bringing an associate with me. Thank you for your cooperation. We will see

170

you this afternoon,' said Paul. He hung up, feeling better about the tape than he had since he found out that it had been stolen.

He told Richard and they were already to leave at one-thirty. The drive was easy and they arrived at the newspaper office fifteen minutes early. They found a café and had a coffee to pass the time. At two-thirty they were in the editor's office and Paul was introducing Richard to Mr Salisbury, the editor.

The editor was staring at Richard as if he knew him and couldn't place him. Richard thought, oh God, don't say he's looked at the tape already. Stupid really. He is the editor of a national newspaper. He's not likely to authorise a payment of the size he just did for something he has not had verified.

They were invited to sit down and Mr Salisbury said to Paul, 'Could you explain to me what all of this is about?'

'I will come straight to the point,' said Paul. 'An aquaintance of mine told me that he had a video tape stolen from his private collection during a burglary. It was the only thing that was taken. The tape is of a sexually explicit nature and could be ruinous to the career of a close friend.'

'Mr Carter,' interrupted the editor.

'Yes,' said Paul. 'The conclusion that was drawn by my friends was that, as that was the only thing taken, there must have been a reason. Scandal. Sell it to the tabloids. You can imagine our surprise when it appeared to have been bought by a newspaper with such a high reputation as yours. We would like it back, together with any other pertinent information you may have received. I'm sure a price can be agreed upon.'

'I do have the tape, which I purchased from a very unsavoury person who sent me an anonymous note. I

171

have seen the tape and, of course, recognised Mr Carter. My children are big fans of *Streetcred*. Nobody else has seen it and I haven't made up my mind what to do with it. As you say, it's not really our sort of journalism. I also have a statement from the young man who supplied me with the tape. In it he says that he lived with you for three months and that he left you when he interrupted you during a sadistic orgy. Is that true?' asked Salisbury.

'Part of it,' said Richard. 'I did live with Todd Jones for a couple of months. *I* was the one who caught him in my house with three other men and I threw them out immediately. I haven't seen him since. Not until yesterday.'

'I had been toying with the idea of doing a feature on pornography – Is it harmful, does it corrupt, does it lead to violence on women, or is it a release for some people? I didn't know enough about the subject to make up my mind whether it could be approached seriously or not. What I wanted was an expert. The arrival of this tape was the answer,' said Salisbury.

'What do you mean?' asked Richard.

'I would like to interview you about your life on the streets,' said the editor.

'I can't believe that I'm hearing this. You want me to go on record saying that I was a rent-boy and a porno star? Do you think I'm mad? I have at last got myself a decent job and I'm beginning to forget about my past, then you ask me to recall what happened. First that tape turns up and now this. I won't do it. It would finish me, and for what, Mr Salisbury?' said Richard.

'No, you don't quite understand. It would be anonymous. What I would like from you are a number of audio tapes, or if you prefer, written stories about your life on the streets. How you first became a rent-boy and how

172

you got into making porn movies. You could send them direct to me. Nobody would need to know who was actually writing them.'

'I'll think about it, after I've got the tape and any letters from Todd.'

'You can have the tape and the letters. I'm serious Mr Carter, I want people to know what goes on, what can happen to their children if they run away to the big city. My son ran off when he was fifteen. He stayed on the streets in London. That's all he will say. He came home after eighteen months. I'm not a fool. I think I know what he was involved in. That's why I want to expose the corruption that takes place almost on a daily basis. Will you help?' said the editor.

'I've said I'll think about it, and I will. Give me time,' said Richard.

'When can I expect an answer from you?' asked Salisbury.

'Within three days,' said Richard.

'Splendid.'

'It's been nice to meet you, Mr Salisbury. This could have been very unpleasant,' said Paul. 'I'll talk to Richard when we get home, but you must realise it will be very hard for him to make public his past, a past which he thought he would be able to forget. Even with anonymity things can be leaked. It doesn't take much for people to add two and two.'

'Yes, I do understand. Goodbye Mr Green, Mr Carter,' said the editor.

Outside the building Richard nearly shouted for joy. 'We did it, we got the tape! Oh Paul, thank God, I was so scared. I had visions of pictures of me on the front page of the papers with really degrading captions.'

173

'What do you think about Salisbury's offer?' asked Paul.

'Can we talk about that later, when I've had time to think it through?' said Richard.

'Sure,' said Paul. 'Let's go home and ring Chris and have a celebratory drink.'

Chris came over and the three of them raised their glasses to toast the successful outcome of the tape fiasco.

'Let's hope we never have to go through this again,' said Chris.

'Hear, hear,' said the other two.

'While we are all together,' said Richard, 'what do you think I should do about Salisbury's feature? If I do it, I think I should insist that no mention of what I'm doing now can appear in any of the articles. I'm still frightened that this could leak to the rest of the press. I had meant to ask Salisbury why Todd had sent the tape to him. Other papers would have been more interested, I'm sure,' said Richard.

'Yes, I've worried about that too,' said Paul. 'Was Todd that much of a fool.'

'Todd Jones is no fool,' said Chris. 'He sent the note to Salisbury deliberately. Perhaps he knew his son. Maybe this was only to be the beginning.'

'I think I'll do his article for him,' said Richard. 'I think I'll also tell John and Alex. After all, Alex knows that I'm gay and I suspect that John does too. I feel a warning about what I used to do is fair.'

'I agree,' said Paul.

'If you're sure kid, I'm behind you. Take care as to what you write. Make sure nothing can be associated with Richard Carter. Dick Hard is the person that you're writing about. It doesn't matter if Salisbury wants every detail,' said Chris.

'OK,' said Richard.

174

The next day Richard asked if he could see John and Alex. He was able to arrange a meeting at two-thirty. He told them how an old friend had been burgled and a video featuring Richard had been stolen. He told them that he had been a rent-boy and had made porno movies. John was staggered. Alex looked as if he wanted to ask Richard a dozen questions. John asked if Paul knew, or if anybody else knew. Richard answered truthfully. He then said what had happened at Salisbury's newspaper office. He explained that he had made up his mind to do what Salisbury wanted, and this was why he had decided to tell John and Alex. It might leak out who Dick Hard was. John listened to the story Salisbury had told about his son and said he understood why Richard felt that he had to do what was being asked of him.

'I think the best thing you can do is to take a couple of months off, to get this whole business out of the way.' John had now cleared the studio of anything connected with Richard Carter or Dick Hard. Richard agreed that this would be the best idea. He said that, all being well, he would call in to see John when he returned from the Seychelles.

Richard told Paul and said that he was going to phone Salisbury and tell him that he would do his story on his terms. The editor happily agreed and Richard started on the project. He started with how he had arrived in London without any money and with nowhere to stay. That was the first mistake runaways make: not having anywhere to stay. He explained how he was taught his trade, without mentioning any names, and how he had gone to posing for gay magazines then on to videos. Richard left out nothing. He sent it to Salisbury. The editor telephoned him the next day, congratulating him

175

on a very sensitive piece. He said he would re-read it and edit a few parts, but basically it would appear as it was in the Thursday edition of the newspaper.

Richard was impatient to see Thursday's paper to see his words in print. He was up early and went to the newsagent's. He returned and went to Paul's room and together they read the feature that Salisbury had written on pornography. It was a very impressive article, but by far the best part was Richard's exposé. It read well and it sounded true. One wanted to know what happened to him. This was something that both Paul and Richard saw and wondered how long it would be before efforts were being made to find out who the author was, and what he was doing now. Richard decided to telephone Alex and ask him if he would have known who the boy in the story was. Alex told him not to worry, he had no idea that it was Richard and could see no reason why anyone should think it was. With relief Richard replaced the phone.

Paul suggested a light lunch in a pub somewhere and then that they should start packing for their holiday.

This they did. They went to bed feeling certain that the article was good and had done its job without exposing Richard as having any part to play in it.

The next morning the papers were full of the feature about the young runaway who had turned to the streets and a life of sex. They all wanted to know who he was and what was he doing now.

Richard went white when he saw the headlines in the tabloids, and was surprised that nearly every paper had something to say about Salisbury's article. Richard showed Paul.

'What are we going to do?' asked Richard.

'We're going to the Seychelles in about four hours,' said Paul. 'When we get back it will all be forgotten.

176

Nobody's going to find out you are the rent-boy. Forget it. Start getting ready. Chris can get in touch with us if any real problems develop.'

'Umm. I hope you're right,' said Richard.

'Aren't I always,' said Paul.

Chapter 12

Chris had spoken to Paul before he and Richard went on holiday. He was as worried as Paul about all the press talk about who was the rent-boy and what was he doing now? Chris knew that when the press got their teeth into something they didn't give up easily, unless something bigger came along. Chris assured Paul that he would keep him up to date with what was happening, and they both agreed to play down any press coverage to Richard.

It seemed that after a couple of days it would all be over. Some newspapers had interviewed boys from the streets to see if what had been said in the paper was an accurate account of their life, and to find out if anyone had any idea of who the rent-boy in the story might be. It appeared to be a very accurate account and the journalists felt that even if the rent-boys did know who the boy was, they were not going to say. As one paper said, 'I interviewed Tom. He's seventeen. I got the impression that he was telling me only as much as he wanted to tell me. If he knew who the boy was he wasn't saying. As far as Tom was concerned, if he'd wanted to have his name in the papers he would have told you himself.' This wasn't looking too bad, thought Chris. It is going to die down through lack of interest. Three days past and mention of the rent-boy story was taking up fewer and fewer column inches.

It was therefore with surprise that at the weekend Chris read an article which gave him a nasty feeling in his stomach. It was an item in a diary column, saying 'could one of our hottest TV stars once have been even hotter in films'? That was all it said, but it was enough to make Chris think that somebody had got a lead on the rent-boy.

The next day the story had a renewed interest. The original paper had more to say about its theory: 'I am told by a reliable source that the real identity of the rent boy is being kept quiet because he is now a reformed person and has been working in TV and films for the past few years.' This, Chris thought, was not true, so at least he hadn't got a really reliable informant. Richard had only worked in TV and had only stopped working for Chris eighteen months ago. Still, it was a bit worrying, as it was near enough to the truth. How long before someone started making it obvious who they were talking about? Perhaps he should telephone Paul.

That evening he went home and rang Paul in the Seychelles. He hoped that Richard would not be there. He dialled the number and waited for what seemed an age before it started to ring. Soon he heard Paul's voice.

'Paul, are you alone? This is Chris.'

'Yes. Richard is still on the beach, he won't be back yet. I take it there's trouble?' asked Paul.

'I'm afraid so. Nothing too bad yet. But the papers are saying that they have a reliable source who tells them that the rent-boy is one of our hottest new TV stars. They're also saying that he has made movies and has

179

been straight for a few years. So I don't know if they are guessing,' said Chris. 'What do you think?'

'I hear what you say. It sounds a bit as though they're making it up, but have got something from someone,' said Paul.

'Yes. I'll keep my eye on things and see how they develop. At the moment I don't think we have anything to worry about. I'll keep you informed. I take it you're having a good time?' said Chris.

'You had better believe it. Richard is wearing me out. It's at times like this that I realise that he's half my age. He's looking wonderful. He's so relaxed, he has a good tan and he's working out on the beach every day with a few other guys who are staying here. He has been introducing me as his step-father. It seemed easier. Well, we'd better say cheers, or your phone bill will be a fortune,' said Paul.

'Yes, you're right. I'll ring again in a couple of days anyway. Have a great time and I'll see you both when you get back. Cheers,' said Chris and hung up.

He had told Paul – that was quite a weight off his shoulders. He was beginning to have a bad feeling that this story was not going to die.

The next morning he scoured the papers for any mention of the story. Nothing. It's over, he thought.

He was filming in the studio that day. As he arrived Chuck was just coming in too.

'Morning, Chris,' said Chuck. 'I've been following the business of the rent-boy story. It sounds to me as though the boy was Dick. Was it, do you know?'

'No, I don't know and I don't want you or anybody else spreading rumours about Richard Carter. Do you understand?' said Chris.

'Sure. I didn't mean to cause any harm, you know that.

180

I wouldn't tell anyone that Dick and I were friends. I liked the guy and, after all, if he hadn't quit I'd still be flexing my pecs for gay magazines,' said Chuck.

Poor Chuck, thought Chris. He wasn't the brightest of people, but he certainly was loyal to his friends. He had liked Richard too, he had forgotten that. 'I'm sorry, Chuck. I didn't mean to yell at you. I know that you'd never say a word to a soul about Richard's past, but I think someone has. I'm just worried who,' said Chris.

'If there's ever anything I can do, you just let me know,' said Chuck.

'I will. For the moment you can get your clothes off. I'm going to start today with some solo spots,' said Chris.

The end of another day, thought Chris. Not a bad day either. Chuck was becoming pretty good and the new boy wasn't bad. I could do with a drink.

Chris packed up and stopped off at the pub on his way home. He ordered a large scotch and sat at a quiet table, lost in his own thoughts. Suddenly he became aware of his surroundings. What had made him conscious of other people? He heard the voice again and knew what it was. Peter le Fenn. He had not heard of him since he fired him after Richard told him he had caught AIDS from him. Chris looked around and there he was, standing by the bar with his back to Chris. He was with two young boys who hardly looked old enough to be in a pub. He listened and could just make out Le Fenn inviting the boys back to his place where they could just have a bit of fun. Chris wanted to go to them and tell them that their new friend had AIDS and wouldn't think twice about passing it on to them. Then it suddenly hit him. Peter le Fenn could be the one informing the press. He had a motive to ruin Richard; he probably needed the money and he had the

181

knowledge. He was also no fool. He would not give any information to a newspaper that could be traced to him by people in the trade, like Chuck. He would feed them the odd bit of disinformation. Chris drank his scotch and left without being seen by Le Fenn.

The newspapers the next day were again speculating about who the rent-boy might be. This time they were talking about a young actor of twenty-six, who had made his debut in a TV series as a streetwise punk. It couldn't have been more obvious that it was Richard Carter. Chris was horrified. He had to ring Paul as soon as possible. They were due home in a couple of days. He rang Paul and told him that it was over. It was now so obvious that the press was referring to Richard, only somebody who had been out of the country for a year would not know the identify of the rent-boy.

That evening on the news there was an item showing John Simmonds being interviewed. John said that he had no knowledge of Richard's past, but found it hard to believe that a guy like Richard could have been involved in such a life.

When the interviewer asked if John had spoken to Richard, he answered that Richard was on holiday in the Seychelles. He also pointed out that technically Richard Carter was nothing to do with his studio as he did not have a contract. New details still had to be worked out and were scheduled for when he returned from holiday.

'Is this still likely to happen?' asked the interviewer.

'I don't know,' said John.

Thank you and goodnight, thought Chris. If that wasn't a kick in the balls, I don't know what is.

The press had a field day with John's interview, saying that they believed that he had known of Richard's past

182

but was trying to hide it. Was it right that someone with a chequered past like Richard's should play the lovable rogue character in *Streetcred*? Suddenly the rent-boy who had everyone's sympathy before his identity was known was the villain of the piece. Chris read all the reports from the papers. All were much the same. Chris knew that the press, smelling blood, would be at the airport to destroy Richard. He had to ring Paul and warn them and tell Paul to prepare Richard. In the meantime Chris was determined to try to find out if Peter le Fenn was in fact the informer, but he didn't quite know how he was going to do that. He would give it some thought.

He slept on the problem, having got hold of Paul and telling him to warn Richard. In the morning he decided to ring the guy who had been writing the stories and asking him if the person from whom he had got his information was Peter le Fenn. He went to the newspaper office. Chris was sure that if they were face to face he stood more chance of getting the truth from the writer. He asked for an appointment and was told eleven-thirty a.m. would be possible. He thanked the secretary and left the building. He phoned Chuck and asked him to hire a car and get to the airport in time to pick up Richard and Paul. He told Chuck that there would be a lot of press presence, all wanting to talk to Richard, and it was his job to stop them and get them away to wherever Paul told him to go, as quickly as he could. Chuck had seen the news and read the papers and understood exactly what he was supposed to do.

Paul and Richard boarded the plane and found their seats. Richard was shocked at what Paul had told him. It hadn't sunk in yet.

'Paul, this is the end for me, isn't it?' asked Richard.

183

'I'd be lying if I said that there's nothing to worry about,' said Paul, grimly.

'I thought things were going too well. I thought John would stand up for me, after all, I did tell him what I was going to do and why. I didn't have to. Even Salisbury hasn't said anything,' said Richard.

'Don't count your chickens, or whatever they say. Remember, if Salisbury says anything it proves that you were the one who wrote the piece. He may want to talk to you first before he says anything to the press. The other thing that I didn't tell you is that Chris thinks he knows who talked – Peter le Fenn.'

'What!' screamed Richard. 'If the bastard isn't happy with giving me a death sentence he now wants to ruin the time I have left. I'll kill him, I swear I'll kill him. After all, what have I got to lose? And think of the pleasure it would give me watching him beg for forgiveness.'

'Calm down,' said Paul. 'You're only drawing attention to yourself. The first thing you've got to do is to be able to cope with the press at the airport. They're going to ask you all sorts of things; probably get at me too.'

'No, Paul, no. I can't let my life affect yours,' said Richard.

'You're too late, son. We've been part of each other's lives for nearly two years now,' said Paul. 'I don't mind. I suggest that you don't say a thing to the press except "no comment", like all good stars. Then I think we should see a solicitor and also talk to Salisbury.'

'Why do you think that I should see a solicitor?' asked Richard, a little dazed.

'It always seems like the thing to do in these circumstances,' said Paul wisely.

'How much longer have we got before landing?' asked Richard.

184

'About two hours. Why don't you try to get some sleep,' said Paul.

'I'll try, but I'm not sure that I'll get any until I know what's going to happen to me,' said Richard.

Poor Richard, thought Paul, he hasn't had a lot of luck. First he has a row with his family, leaves, and that goes wrong. Nobody came to look for him. He finishes up on the streets and catches AIDS – hardly surprising I suppose. He, then, through his own ability and hard work, gets a good job and becomes a star. With that comes the loss of privacy. Would the press have cared if a rent-boy had told his story but had still been carrying on with his trade? No. It's the fact that he's made good and become part of the establishment that interests the press. That's the sin and so now he will have to suffer public exposure of his past life and, what's more, ruin his current life. The poor little sod, I wish I could put my arms around him now, but I'd better not.

The lights came on and the purser announced that they were beginning the descent to Gatwick. Paul nudged Richard.

'For one who would never sleep again you didn't do too bad,' grinned Paul.

'You know me, have my fun and then all I want to do is sleep. Can't help it,' smiled Richard. 'How much longer?'

'I suppose about twenty minutes,' said Paul, 'Come on, we can take on the world while we're together. Just remember what I said, don't say anything except no comment.'

The plane landed. They disembarked and started to move towards passport control. From there they walked to the baggage collection, and then it happened. The arrival area was full of press photographers and newsmen screaming like a pack of animals. It was not only Richard and Paul who couldn't get through, it was the other passengers too. In all the confusion Richard heard someone call his name, and it was a voice that he recognised. It was Chuck. He looked around and spotted him behind a screen at the back of the exit. Richard grabbed Paul and dragged him towards Chuck. Chuck picked up the luggage and pushed Richard and Paul into the car that he had waiting. It had cost him a few quid to bribe the security staff, but as they saw the press arrive they felt it might be for the best.

'Where do you want to go?' asked Chuck. 'Chris told me to take you to wherever Paul told me to go.'

'Chuck, I can't believe this, I'm so grateful. You don't know how scared I was of all those press guys. Paul, Chuck and I used to work together.' Richard introduced them.

'How are you?' said Paul. 'I'm glad you arrived too. How did you manage to get the car parked there?'

Chuck looked at Richard and winked. 'We have ways of making some guys do anything we want,' said Chuck.

'Oh,' said Paul, suddenly catching on and turning slightly red.

'Where do you want to go?'

'If they're not following us I don't see why we can't go home. So to Hounslow please, Chuck,' said Paul lightly.

'OK,' said the big guy, who was obviously pleased to have been able to help. 'I just want to say, Dick . . . I'm sorry, *Richard*, that the word on the streets is that you have had a rotten deal. They don't like it, and if they find out who talked they'll be dead meat.'

'Thanks, Chuck. That's the best bit of news that I've heard for a long time,' said Richard.

'Turn left here, Chuck, it's just round to your right,' said Paul.

'Do you want to come in for a drink? You can have coffee if you like as you're driving,' offered Paul.

'No, I won't, thank you, Paul. I've got to get the car back by seven or I'm in for another day's rent,' said Chuck.

'Thanks a lot, Chuck – for everything. We must meet up for a drink sometime,' said Richard.

'Yes,' said Chuck. 'We must try to arrange it.' Chuck knew that it would be most unlikely that he and Richard would meet for anything. He was not in the same business now and so they had nothing in common.

'Cheerio,' said Paul.

They watched him drive off. Paul said, 'You've got some good friends.'

'Yes,' said Richard, 'one of the best of them is standing next to me now.' Richard put his arms round Paul's shoulders. 'Come on, let's phone Chris and find out what's been going on. I could seriously use a drink too.'

'Agreed. I've never been so frightened as I was when I saw those pressmen screaming at you. I felt so intimidated. God knows what would have happened if Chuck hadn't turned up. We must remember to thank Chris for that piece of forethought, and perhaps we can arrange for Chuck to have a bonus,' said Paul.

Richard laughed, 'The only bonus you could give Chuck is more of the same. He loves screwing men, he can't get enough of it.'

'I see, anyway, let's phone Chris,' said Paul.

Chris arrived at eight-thirty. He looked worried and as if he had not had any sleep for a while.

'Hi, you look as if you could do with a drink,' said Paul.

'You're a gentleman. Can I have a scotch and water? I have had a hell of a day,' said Chris.

'Ours has been fairly uneventful,' said Richard with a smirk.

'Did Chuck get to the airport on time?' asked Chris.

'He was a star. He turned up on time and he'd bribed the security staff to let him park at the back of the exit and he managed to sneak us away without the press really knowing, although they were all howling like wolves as we disappeared. Paul wants you to give him a bonus,' said Richard. 'I told him the only bonus that would please Chuck would be more of the same. He's insatiable, isn't he.'

'Yes. Almost as bad as you,' said Chris, as Richard threw a cushion at him. 'Only joking.'

Paul gave Chris his drink. 'Well, you had better tell us exactly what's been going on while we have been away. It won't be long before the press is camped out here.'

'I told you that I saw Peter le Fenn and I had a hunch that he had something to do with the renewed interest in the story. I decided to find out. I made an appointment with the journalist who had written the piece practically identifying you, Richard. I saw him today. I asked him outright if he was getting his information from someone called Peter le Fenn, but he refused to name his source. They're so bloody moral these journalists when it comes to naming their source. It's a pity they don't apply the same morals to what they write. Anyway, I said that I had a pretty good idea that it was him because some of the facts were slightly wrong. I told this guy that I knew Le Fenn and that I had fired him because he had AIDS and hadn't told anybody. He had by now guessed my line of business. I told him that there was more to the rent-boy story than meets the eye. I explained that you had been on holiday and that until you were back and had spoken to Salisbury nothing more would be said.

'I told the guy to lay off, at least until you had had a chance to talk to Salisbury. I also told him that some of what he had printed was libellous – that he should check his facts more thoroughly. That bothered him and he agreed not to print another word on the story for a maximum of three days. I took the liberty of ringing Salisbury on your behalf, Richard. I asked him why he hadn't written something in his paper to explain why you had agreed to write the piece in the first place. If you hadn't agreed, you wouldn't be in the position you are in now. Salisbury said he had tried to phone you, but, of course, you were on holiday. He didn't want to say anything without talking to you first. As soon as he reveals the reason why you agreed to write the piece it confirms the rumours that Richard Carter was in fact Dick Hard. I told him that you were due back from the Seychelles today and made an appointment for you to see him tomorrow. I hope that's all right,' said Chris.

'Chris, you are a genius. Paul and I had spoken on similar lines on the plane home. I think if we can get Salisbury to give us some sympathetic press and we can stop the other guy writing Le Fenn's lies this might blow over. What do you think, Paul?' asked Richard.

'I certainly think it'll help, but don't get too excited. I want to speak to my so-called friend John. I think the way he dumped you is disgraceful. Particularly as you had the guts to tell him everything beforehand,' said Paul.

'We were also talking about going to a solicitor,' said Richard. 'Do you think that it's still necessary?'

'I would if I were you,' said Chris. 'A lot of things have

been written in the press over the last few weeks and if this does cause your career to tumble, well, you'll have a clear-cut case, I would say, to claim for damages, substantial damages too. Your career was definitely on the way up. One of the first things to connect you with the story was the reference to TV's hottest new star.'

'I agree' said Paul. 'We'll go to see Salisbury tomorrow morning and then go to my solicitor and explain the entire episode to him.'

'At some stage tomorrow I want to go to the studio. I said I would call in when I got back from holiday. They might have some work for me,' said Richard.

'Let's see what Salisbury and the solicitor have to say first,' said Paul. 'You're not broke yet, are you?'

'Nearly,' grinned Richard. 'It's not that – I must find out for myself how people are going to react to me now that my wicked past is public knowledge.'

'I wouldn't build your hopes high. People can be funny, and if there's a vocal minority against you that will swing the rest. Remember Kate Stevens? How do you think she's reacting to this?' asked Paul.

'I should think she's loving it,' said Richard, 'but what about Alex and Michael? I can't believe either of them will abandon me.'

'Why don't you ring Michael and ask him how the land lies if that'll put your mind at rest,' said Paul.

'Yes, good idea,' said Richard, getting up to go to the phone.

'Not now, boy. Look at the time. Ring him in the morning,' said Paul. Chris laughed. 'He always was perpetual motion.'

'He exhausts me sometimes,' said Paul.

'Shall we have one last drink and call it a day? You can stay the night if you wish, Chris. You can have my room.

190

Paul and I can share for one night. I'll try not to exhaust you too quickly,' said Richard.

'Cheeky,' said Paul. 'Yes, that's fine by me. It is late and we've had a few to many for driving anyway.'

'Thanks, if it's no trouble,' said Chris.

'Richard has been working on some way of getting into my bed for the last two years. Let him have his night of fantasy,' grinned Paul.

Paul and Richard went into Salisbury's office and sat down. His secretary had said that he wouldn't be long. They had both declined coffee. The door opened and Salisbury entered.

'Good morning, gentlemen. I'm sorry that our next meeting should be under these circumstances. Sometimes I despair of some of my fellow journalists. I did try to telephone you, Mr Carter, when the first innuendo appeared in the press. I now understand that you were on holiday. I didn't want to add anything that would fuel the fire before I had spoken to you. If I print your reasons for helping me with my feature on pornography I would be virtually confirming the rumours. How do you feel about that?'

'I am quite happy for you to confirm them, Mr Salisbury. In fact, what I would like to suggest is that I write a few words confirming that I am, or was, Dick Hard and why I agreed to put my career at risk. I think that between us we can show that even if you are caught up in the underworld of dirty movies it is possible to get out and start a new life. I think it's pointless now my pretending that Dick Hard doesn't exist,' said Richard.

'I'm very pleased to hear you say that because it's exactly what I had in mind. Incidentally, I am pleased to say that my son has at last told us what happened to him.

191

He said it was your part of the article that made him realise that it would always be a part of his life, not a part that he was proud of, but he would feel better if he spoke about it to someone. He said that he thought about going to a counsellor, but in the end decided to talk to me. I was so proud of him at that moment. He's more relaxed now and is beginning to take an interest in life,' said Mr Salisbury.

'I'm very pleased for you,' said Paul. 'At least some good has come out of all of this.'

'I hope a lot more will too,' said Salisbury.

'Yes. Richard has still to find out if he's employable. The way things have been going in the press recently he may have a very limited career. Pervert or perhaps a rapist,' said Paul.

'Paul, I don't think it is that bad, and I don't think Mr Salisbury can do any more to help,' said Richard.

'I hope you still feel so generous in six months, Richard.'

'We can talk about that later. Shall I write my "confession" and post it to you?' asked Richard.

'Yes, if you would. I am sorry about the way this has turned out for you. If there is anything I can do I will,' said Salisbury. He stood up to show his guests out. They shook hands and left.

The next stop was the solicitor's. Paul did most of the talking and explained who Richard was and what he had just agreed to write for Salisbury. The solicitor agreed that if Richard's career suffered unduly in the near future they did stand a good chance of getting compensation. Whom they decided to sue they would look at later. John Simmonds seemed a prime target after the way he had spoken on television. The solicitor said he would start gathering all of the old newspapers with anything written about the

192

story or any allusion to Richard. They agreed to meet in a week's time.

Richard wanted to speak to Michael. As it was nearly lunchtime Paul looked for a pub where they could eat and Richard could phone.

Richard phoned the studio and asked for Michael.

'Hi, Michael. It's Richard. How are things? What's happening at the old place and what's the gossip about me?'

'Richard, I can't talk to you here. Can I meet you sometime, tonight, in our pub?'

'Yes OK, at six-thirty. Is it that bad?'

'Yes,' he hung up.

When they got home Richard told Paul he was going to write his article for Salisbury. He went into the lounge and started to write.

My name is Richard Carter. Yes, the recent speculation in the press as to my being the rent-boy in Gerald Salisbury's feature on pornography is correct. I agreed to write the piece on my terms, which were anonymity, because I felt then, and still do, that what Gerald Salisbury is trying to explain is the danger young people can find themselves in when they run away from home to live in major cities. I also wrote about myself in such a frank way because I also believe that you can reverse the trend of a life on the streets, and can find yourself a career to help make you into a useful member of society. What you need is a friend. I was very lucky. The friend I met has stood by me through all of the bad times as well as the good. It isn't easy to give up being a prostitute – that applies to men as well as women. Former associates have to be erased from your new social life. It's a different life and different values

193

apply. Every effort has to be made by the reformer to become acceptable in his new world.

The risks of trading on the streets are enormous. Drug addiction and AIDS are commonplace. This makes you extremely vulnerable. Violence is now a way of life for some members of our society, which means that rape, both male and female rape, and murder, are crimes that could happen to the rent-boy at any time.

I decided to tell my story because I know that some youngsters are reading this now and know exactly what I am saying because they have been there. What they haven't been able to do is talk to anyone about their experiences. Gerald Salisbury's son was one of those people. Mr Salisbury told me that his son had left home at fifteen and had spent eighteen months on the streets in London. He had not said one word of what had happened to him. That is until he read the feature his father had written. The boy then wanted to talk to his father, not a counsellor, his father. Mr Salisbury is proud of his son. He, at a very impressionable age, went through the horrors that I went through. He felt ashamed and disgusted with himself. He couldn't recognise that his feelings of guilt and shame would be easier to bear if he spoke to someone that he loved.

I know what I did when I came to London was wrong and certainly foolish. I have paid the price for my stupidity. The ultimate price: I am HIV positive. I was infected by someone who knew that he had the disease, but chose not to tell me. I may live ten years; I may live two. Only God knows the answer to that. I agreed to write this piece for Gerald Salisbury because I don't want youngsters ruining their lives because they think it will never happen to them. It does.'

Richard read what he had written, put it into an envelope ready to post when he went to meet Michael.

Michael was waiting for Richard when he arrived.

'I'm sorry I'm a bit late,' said Richard. 'How are you? Good, I hope. And what the hell is happening at the studio? I was going to see Alex tomorrow, but after what you said I began to wonder.'

'Richard, it's terrible. That bitch Kate is stirring up everybody. She says that we should fire you and disassociate the studio from your name. She reckons that we should put out a public apology for ever having cast you in *Streetcred*,' said Michael.

'What, she can't do that! She must be mad. What about other people, Alex, for example, or John?' asked Richard.

'The closet gays are all behaving in a very macho way – it's pathetic. The gays are keeping their heads down. We need our jobs. I don't know why Kate is the way she is. After all, before she found out about you I thought she was going to try to bed you,' said Michael.

'She did.'

'What are you going to do?' asked Michael. 'If there is anything I can do to help you know I will, within reason,' he added quietly.

'I know, Michael. I do understand your position and the other guys. I don't want you compromising yourselves for me. Tomorrow there will be another article in the press written by me explaining why I did what I did. I'm hoping that it'll calm things down and maybe even put a few people on my side. Paul and I have been to a solicitor, and he thinks that I have a good case for compensation if my career suffers. I think Paul is going to see John in the morning. They were old friends; I'm not so sure now. I am going to try to see Alex. I must find out why Kate is being such a cow. It's crazy,' said Richard.

195

'The best of luck,' said Michael. 'Can I buy you a drink?'

'Cheers, I'll have a pint of bitter,' said Richard.While Michael was at the bar, Mandy and two other cast members from *Streetcred* came into the bar.

'Richard, I didn't expect to see you here. You're a brave guy. If Kate sees you she'll kill you in front of everybody,' said Mandy.

'What is it with her? Why is she so anti-gay? In her job it seems illogical. She must meet dozens a week,' said Richard.

'I think she had a bad experience with a gay once,' said Mandy.

'What do you mean, she fell for him?' asked Richard.

'I think so, but that's all I know,' said Mandy.

'Michael has been telling me what it's like in the studio. Where do you and the rest of the cast stand?' asked Richard.

'I, like everybody else in this selfish business, am trying to look after number one. If you want to know how I really feel, I think it's all a lot of fuss about nothing. But I do think you're a fool. You must have known that there would be an outcry from the press. What made you do it?' asked Mandy.

'Read tomorrow's papers to find the answer,' said Richard smiling.

'You haven't said any more, have you,' asked Mandy, astounded that he could be so foolish, in her eyes anyway.

'Yes. I had no alternative. The tabloids were all but naming me as the rent-boy in the original story and they were printing facts that were not true. I had to admit that I was Dick Hard,' said Richard.

'I love that name,' said Mandy.

'Yes, I bet you do – and reversed,' said Richard.

196

'Pity you're gay. We could have had a hell of a time, I bet.'

'*C'est la vie*,' said Richard.

'Hi, Mandy,' said Michael. 'I've been trying to tell Richard what it's like back at the factory. It's scary, isn't it?'

'Yes, I suppose it is really,' said Mandy. 'What are you going to do, Richard?' she asked.

'I'm not sure, but I do intend to fight for my honour,' Richard smiled. 'I've put too much into this career to quit now just because of some crazy, homophobic middle-aged woman!'

'You could be what is needed to bring people back from the brink and to look at things rationally. You have to admit, it was a bit of a shock for most of us. I'll admit that some got closer to you than others, didn't they, darling?' she said grinning at Michael.

'You don't always get first go at the men, you know, Mandy,' said Michael.

Richard laughed. 'I'm going, or I'll get picked up for drunken driving. I'll see you all tomorrow, I think.'

'Bye, Richard,' said Michael, still with the adoring expression on his face.

Todd Jones was still recovering from the beating that he had received from Richard. He was not seriously injured, except perhaps for his ego. He was reading the paper and was surprised to see that the story of the rent-boy was in the news again. He read the article that the editor had written to supplement Richard's piece. He was angry at the sympathy for Richard coming from the editor. I'll show him, thought Todd. No one beats up on Todd Jones like that and gets away with it. Todd picked up the phone and dialled the phone number of the paper that had first

197

suggested that Richard Carter and Dick Hard were the same person. He asked for the Diary Editor.

'Yes, can I help you?' said a voice.

'I think I can help *you*. Have you seen the article by Gerald Salisbury in today's paper?' asked Todd.

'If you mean the one on Richard Carter, yes. It only goes to show that we were right all along,' answered the voice.

'I think Carter has been put in a very good light. He's shown to be a saint. I know that he isn't,' said Todd.

'What do you know?'

'I know that Richard Carter beat me half to death and left me unconscious to get information from me,' said Todd.

'Who are you?' asked the voice.

'That doesn't matter. If you're interested in bringing Mr Richard Carter down to the gutter where he belongs, I'll give you the details and you can check them with the hospital,' said Todd.

'Yes, I'm very interested.'

'Good. When can I meet you? Today would be fine for me,' said Todd.

'I can see you at eleven o'clock in the Red Lion, it's just . . .'

'I know where it is,' interrupted Todd. 'I'll see you there. Don't be late.' Todd hung up.

What a thoroughly unpleasant person, thought Colin, the Diary Editor. He made a note in his diary: 'Red Lion, 11.' He read Richard's piece again. This time he was thinking about what the guy had said. He left me unconscious, he beat me half to death. I think I must meet Mr Carter. The way I feel about the creep who just phoned me, I would think he deserved a beating.

Richard went to the studio as if everything was back to normal. He said 'hello' to the receptionist and walked into the lift to go to Alex's office. He asked Alex's secretary if Alex was free and could he see him for a few minutes. She checked and asked Richard to go in.

'Richard! I didn't expect to see you,' said Alex.

'Hello, Alex, why not? I said I would be in when I got back from holiday. Here I am,' said Richard.

Alex was beginning to look flustered. 'I thought you said you would be away until all of this business of the rent-boy had died down.'

'Alex, things have changed since I went away. I was all but named in the press. John dropped me on a TV interview. I phoned Michael and he told me that it was hell here. Kate was going mad and wanted all gays' balls – preferably before the end of the week. I don't know if you've read the paper today, but I've written another article confirming that I am Dick Hard and giving my reasons for agreeing to write for Gerald Salisbury.'

Alex looked at Richard. His mouth was open as though he couldn't believe what he had just heard. 'You've done what?'

'Why don't you send for a copy of the paper and read it for yourself,' suggested Richard.

'Yes, I will.' Alex buzzed his secretary and asked her to bring him all of that morning's papers. 'What made you do that? Surely by admitting that you were the rent-boy you've really screwed your career,' said Alex.

'That's what I want to find out from you and John,' said Richard. 'I agreed to write that article for the best of reasons. People are still so prejudiced that they're more interested in naming me and trying to ruin my life. Alex, you knew I was gay before any of this press coverage. What's the difference. I am still the same person and I didn't try to hide anything from you or John. I even told you the full story before the event so that you could be prepared if any adverse publicity fell on the studio. I didn't have to do that, you know – you owe me one,' said Richard.

'It's not quite so easy. John has worked with Kate for years, he trusts her judgement. She would like to see you fry.'

'What is her problem? She's a modern woman and on most other subjects she takes the liberal stance. Why is she so uptight about homosexuality? After all, it's something that she need never involve herself in. Not many gays go around forcing themselves on straights.'

The secretary brought in the papers.

'Let me read this new article of yours,' said Alex. 'Have some coffee.'

Richard poured a cup of coffee for them both and sat and watched Alex's face as he read the article. He knew by the time that he had finished he had got Alex back on his side. He would have to work on Kate, but that wasn't going to be easy. Perhaps he should try John next.

Alex put the paper down. 'I'm feeling somewhat ashamed and not a little bit foolish. I'm also very sorry Richard to hear that you are HIV positive.'

'Thanks. Does that mean that I've got my job back?' asked Richard.

'Let's take this slowly. I don't think you can play Tony again. The image that we created for him won't work now. I'll think about it and talk to John,' said Alex.

'Fair enough,' said Richard smiling. 'I'll see you tomorrow.'

'We are still friends, aren't we,' asked Alex. 'Because there are lots of things I want to talk to you about. I thought maybe we could go for a weekend to the coast sometime.'

'Sorry, Alex. Weekends are out. Paul is my weekend friend. If you want to talk about anything that I've written or implied in the articles, that's different. Any time and in private, but not in a bedroom,' said Richard.

Richard left Alex's office and tried to find Kate. He might as well get it over with. He went to her office, but she wasn't there. He looked for her on the set, but no. He tried the make-up department and she was there. She was being particularly abusive to Michael.

'I'm here now, Kate. Why don't you take your venom out on me?' said Richard.

'You? What are you doing here?' said Kate.

'I want to make sure that I still have a job,' said Richard.

'Ha! You must think we're all mad to employ someone like you.'

'I did when you first hired me. I had no experience of acting – no formal training. You though, Kate, said that I had sex appeal and that look that you hadn't been able to find in anybody else. I'm the same person. You know more about me now, but it's in my past. I accept that I couldn't play Tony again. The image is all wrong, and too near the truth,' said Richard.

'You'll never work anywhere again if I have my way,' declared Kate.

'What is it in your past that has made you feel like this, Kate? You're fortunate to have been able to keep your past to yourself. I tried, but couldn't. I told Alex and John all about myself and what I was going to write before I went on holiday, so it couldn't have been such a shock. Surely, they told you? After all, you're so close to John,' said Richard.

'My past is my business. It's got nothing to do with

201

you. Get out. I don't want to see you here again!' said Kate, close to tears.

'I don't think that that is up to you, darling,' said Richard. 'I'll see you tomorrow.'

'Michael, we must make arrangements for dinner one night. I know Paul would like to see you again,' said Richard.

'Thanks, Richard. That would be good. Say hello to Paul for me,' said Michael.

Richard decided that he could do no more fighting for his job today. He felt tired and a little exhausted. He rang Alex and said that he was going home if he wanted him. He drove out to Hounslow with his mind in turmoil. He thought he had won Alex over to his side. The press article he had written as Richard Carter had helped. Kate he still could not understand. Something was blocking her normal sense of fair play. The rest of the staff seemed all right. Maybe it would work out in the end. The end – he hoped that this was the end. Nothing else could keep the press interested. He parked his car in the drive. Paul did not appear to be in. Good, he thought. I just want to lie down for a while, perhaps have a little sleep. Richard went to his room and within three or four minutes he was fast asleep.

Paul arrived home at six p.m. He looked about for Richard. He knew he was home as his car was blocking the drive again. He called a couple of times and got no response. He eventually went to Richard's room and looked in. Richard was asleep on top of the bed. He looked drawn and tired and he appeared to have lost weight. Paul decided to leave him.

He phoned Chris and told him that he had seen John Simmonds. He said he thought John had behaved pretty badly towards Richard. They got things sorted out and

Richard still had a job. Paul said that he thought that the article explaining why he wrote the first article had helped. Chris agreed it was a good piece of work. Where was the boy now, asked Chris. When Paul told him he was in bed and explained how he looked Chris sounded worried and asked if Paul thought he might really be ill with AIDS.

Paul was shocked. Of course, he knew that one day something like this could happen. But not yet, not to Richard. He was so young. He had a life just beginning and he had been fighting for it so hard lately. He couldn't be ill now. Chris said he would call tomorrow to see how Richard was feeling.

'Richard Carter beat me half to death and left me unconscious.'

That was the headline that Colin had used to regain the readers in the battle of Richard Carter. Colin realised that after the explanation as to why he had exposed himself as a rent-boy and porno star, he would be Mr Nice Guy again. The article went on to tell how, according to an unnamed source, Richard Carter had gone to his flat and intimidated him and beat him because he had heard that a tape featuring him as Dick Hard had been sold to the newspapers. His source claimed that Carter would not stop hitting him until he said which newspaper had the tape.

Paul saw the item and thought, oh no, here we go again. Todd Jones, of course. He had conveniently forgotten that the tape had been a stolen tape and that he, Jones, had stolen it. Paul suddenly thought, what if the paper persuades Todd to sue Richard for assault? Chris could tell

203

the police that the tape had been stolen in the first place; from him.

Paul became aware that he hadn't heard Richard moving about and yet he had said he was going to the studio. He knocked on the door to his room and went in. What he saw frightened him. Richard was lying on the bed, he was sweating and his eyes looked blank as though he couldn't see. His breathing was laboured.

'Richard. For God's sake, what's wrong?' asked Paul.

'I don't know, Paul, but I don't feel very well. I don't think I'll go to the studio today. Do you think you could call a doctor?' asked Richard.

'Certainly I will. You try to drink some of this water and I'll get you some more pyjamas, those are soaking wet,' said Paul. He found Richard some fresh clothes and changed them for him. He also phoned the doctor, explaining the circumstances. Then he rang Chris and gave him an update. Chris said he would be round in half an hour. Paul returned to Richard with a damp cloth to mop his forehead. Richard seemed to be asleep.

The doctor confirmed what Paul had thought. 'I can't be certain without further tests, but as Mr Carter is HIV positive it's almost certain that he now has full-blown AIDS. I read the papers too, Mr Green. I know how much stress Richard has been under. Something like that could trigger the disease. I must say, I admire him for what he has done. First to change his lifestyle, then to tell the truth about himself to help others understand what they are getting into, and to finally identify himself not as a new young star of television but as the rent-boy and porno star of the article. He also admitted that he was HIV positive. I don't know about that, but he has got a hell of a lot of guts. I wonder if he learnt it on the streets.'

'What happens now?' asked Paul.

204

'I'll have to have my diagnosis confirmed and then arrange to have him transferred to hospital,' said the doctor.

'Can he stay here?' asked Paul.

'No, not yet. He can be treated and could well recover from this, as he is a strong lad. If it does get to that stage, are you willing to have him staying with you, Mr Green?'

'Yes. I wouldn't have it any other way,' said Paul. 'I don't want him to go to a hospice, but I'll leave the timing to you. I just want the best for Richard.'

'He will get that, don't worry too much,' said the doctor.

The doorbell rang.

'I'll be off to make the arrangements. You'll be hearing from me soon.'

Paul opened the door to see the doctor out and Chris was waiting to come in. When Paul returned to the lounge Chris asked, 'Is it the worst?'

'He thinks so, but has to be confirmed with further tests. He looks awful, Chris. The doctor thinks that all the publicity and the resultant stress could have triggered the disease,' said Paul. 'Come and see him.'

Chris was visibly shocked at Richard's appearance. How could anyone change so quickly?

Later Paul read the article Richard had written under the pseudonym Dick Hard, which had caused so much devastation to so many lives.

I arrived in London a little more than ten years ago, I was sixteen and a half. I had just enough money to buy a hamburger and a hot drink. I didn't have any idea where I was going to sleep or how I was going to earn money to feed myself in the future. It didn't take me long to find out. A lad only a few years older than me asked if I needed help. We arranged that I could sleep on his couch for a few days, but I would have to earn some money to help with the rent. I readily accepted, not knowing how I was going to have to earn the money. I was taught my trade well. I soon found clients were willing to pay for my services. Hanging around main-line stations and certain other areas of London I could easily earn money as a rent-boy. Once entangled with the pimps, whores and junkies, who are also part of this underworld, it's hard to break away. If you can manage to stay off drugs, keep your body in trim and keep your looks, it's likely that you will become a model. Posing nude for gay magazines can be very lucrative. Although I repeatedly told myself that as soon as I had enough money I would be out of this. I never seemed to manage it. I graduated to making pornographic videos. Gay porn appears to be a fast growing industry.

Two years ago I did manage to start a new life. I met someone who believed in me. Someone that I could talk to, who would listen to me. I know that my past has not been the way most people live, and I'm not proud of it. But I know a lot of people who have done a lot worse: drug dealers, rapists, child abusers; some of the girls who work the streets have been beaten half to death by their pimps who thought the girls were cheating on them. As a rent-boy my customers came to me, I didn't tout for business. They knew where to look. As a porno star I was working with other people like me, who knew what they were doing. We didn't hurt ourselves or each other. Gay porn is sold to those who want to watch it in private, not for them to corrupt their neighbours. If society wants to stop our youngsters becoming rent-boys and prostitutes maybe it should look at why fifteen- and sixteen-year-olds are leaving home for the big cities. If society doesn't want rent-boys, cut down on the raw material.

Paul put the article down. He wondered what would have happened to Richard if they had never met. Would he have tried to quit working for Chris? Would he have carried on doing what he was good at until he could do it no more? Who knows. Who knew what had been the best for Richard now. Paul went to look in on him. Richard was asleep. Paul looked at him and remembered how he had thought of him as a modern-day Adonis. He was beautiful. Now his face was gaunt, his eyes had sunk into his head. His muscular body looked almost skeletal. It was a tragedy. Paul wondered how much of this he could take. He thought of something he had said when he retired. 'The trouble is I'm gay.' Does that mean that you deserve to die like this?